IF ALL ELSE FAILS

IF ALL ELSE FAILS

THE KURTHERIAN ENDGAME™ - OUT OF TIME
BOOK TWO

ND ROBERTS

MICHAEL ANDERLE

DISRUPTIVE IMAGINATION

Copyright © 2019 N.D. Roberts and Michael Anderle
Cover by Andrew Dobell, www.creativeedgestudios.co.uk
Cover copyright © LMBPN Publishing
Interior Images by Eric Quigley
Interior Images © LMBPN Publishing
This book is a Michael Anderle Production

LMBPN Publishing
PMB 196, 2540 South Maryland Pkwy
Las Vegas, NV 89109

First US edition, December, 2019
eBook ISBN: 978-1-64202-608-5
Print ISBN: 978-1-64202-609-2

IF ALL ELSE FAILS TEAM

Thanks to our Beta Readers:
Diane Velasquez, Dorene Johnson, USNR, and
Timothy Cox

Thanks to the JIT Readers

Dave Hicks
Diane L. Smith
Misty Roa
Jackey Hankard-Brodie
Dorothy Lloyd
John Ashmore
Daniel Weigert
Peter Manis
Jeff Goode
Kelly O'Donnell
Deb Mader
Micky Cocker
Jeff Eaton
James Caplan

If I've missed anyone, please let me know!

Editor
Lynne Stiegler

DEDICATION

For the children we all are in our hearts.

— Nat

To Family, Friends and
Those Who Love
To Read.
May We All Enjoy Grace
To Live The Life We Are
Called.

—Michael

CHAPTER ONE

The Corral, Parade Ground

One moment Gabriel was calling one last goodbye to his parents, and the next, he was standing at ease on the parade ground with Alexis, Trey, and K'aia around him.

No integration scenario? K'aia murmured over the team link. *My stomachs aren't too happy about that.*

The neural integration was done on the first insertion, Alexis ventured. *There was no need for the scenario. I'm not in the mood for fun and games, anyway.*

Gabriel shrugged minutely. *It doesn't feel right to take this lightly anymore. We have to focus on making every day count.* There was no joy in play while his heart was still weighted by the loss of his aunt.

Relax, K'aia told them gently. *Otherwise, all you'll end up doing is going around in circles until your brains explode. I can't believe I'm saying this, but you could learn something from Trey. His clowning got him through some dark times.*

Hey! Trey resisted narrowing his eyes, knowing better than to move a muscle while the SIs were watching for the

1

slightest infraction. *I'm a finely-tuned sarcasm machine, thank you.*

Alexis let the conversation wash around her. She found the immediate reinsertion somewhat jarring. More so when General Kispin's booming voice rang out, causing every recruit, including her, to twitch involuntarily.

The general stood at ease, unbothered by the volume of his parade voice. "Congratulations on passing basic training. You have all been promoted to corporal, and will have the opportunity to advance to specialist should you continue to prove your worth going forward." A look that could possibly be interpreted as fondness contorted his horned face into a tight rictus. "Many stood here on intake day. You twenty are all who remain at the end of basic training. You have been broken and rebuilt into something stronger. Those of differing abilities have been filtered out and reassigned according to their talents. This process has cut away the weak, the easily injured, and the self-oriented."

General Kispin glanced at the SIs. "Some of those being instructing officers."

The remaining SIs stared straight ahead. Not so much as an eyelid twitched at the general's remark.

Trey snickered over the team link. *They look so uptight. I bet they'd explode before they dared so much as fart.*

Wouldn't you be? K'aia asked. *The general tossed the others out on their asses for abusing their positions. How do you think the rejects are doing out on the front line of this war?*

He's not done talking, Gabriel told them. *Quiet for a minute. It would be just like us to miss something that would help us later on because we weren't paying attention.*

The general dragged his stern gaze from the staff instructors and returned his attention to the new soldiers on parade. "This is your last day at the Corral. You will strip your barracks and return everything with the exception of the uniform you are wearing to the requisitions building. Then you will be taken to your transport and placed in stasis for the journey. Zenith Station awaits. Leave here with pride, knowing that you beat almost insurmountable odds to make it to this stage. You are the best, and you will be made better still in the months to come."

He gave the order to fall out and two of the SIs moved to direct the twenty corporals, regardless of the need for it.

"It's another story for the recruits who didn't make the final cut," Alexis grumbled as she trudged into the barracks behind Trey. "They don't get special assignments or opportunities. They get shipped to the battle zone and thrown in to fight or die whether they wanted to be soldiers or not."

Sibil's hissing laughter sounded strange in the almost empty room. "What in the universe are you talking about? *Nobody* except for you four *wanted* to be here. Why would anyone in their right mind leave a safe planet and look for a fight? Not me, that's for sure."

Gabriel noted the shift in the color of Sibil's scales, which indicated she was holding back. He grinned at his reptilian friend. "But?"

Sibil shrugged, her scales flushing further as the blood rushed to her face. "I dunno. I like being able to fight for myself for a change. I can see it as a fair exchange to give a few years of service in return."

"I don't get why anyone would want to turn down the

chance for glory," Trey cut in. "Whatever battles we fight will add to the stories the poets tell about our lives."

"I wanted to be a poet," Gorrak admitted reluctantly. "But I never learned to write. There aren't many schools for Shrillexians with creative minds. Plenty of fight clubs, though."

"You're not exactly shy when there's a fight on offer," Sibil told him with a soft smile. She turned her back to the group while she stripped the sheets from her bunk. "I wonder why we're going into stasis again?"

Trey picked up his folded bundle. "Zenith Station must be pretty far from here."

Last time we went into stasis, Trey got a boost. Alexis placed her pillow on top of her pile and picked it up. *I'm guessing we're about to have another growth spurt, and Eve has to put us all the way under.*

About time, Gabriel stated quietly. *I hope Eve is finished with the aging part of the enhancement when we get there. I'm really done feeling like a cookie that got taken out of the oven half-baked.*

K'aia was also feeling introspective. *I'm having second thoughts about this enhancement. I don't know if I want to live forever. What do people who live forever even do with all that time?*

Ask us in a thousand years, Gabriel teased.

The same officer who had handed out their gear took it back without preamble and moved the line along with a disinterested wave.

K'aia was still quiet as they returned to the parade ground, where their transport to the stasis ship was just landing on the gravel.

The SIs who had supervised the gear return gave the order for them to line up for boarding.

Are you really feeling doubtful? Alexis asked as they entered the personnel bay aboard the carrier. *You can always have your nanocytes switched off if you want to settle down.*

You can? K'aia glanced at Gabriel. *I've never heard of anyone doing that.*

Gabriel shrugged and took a seat on the left-hand bench. *Me either. Mom would know.*

If you want it reversed, I'll find a way, Alexis promised, placing her hand on K'aia's arm. *You know that. But I can't reverse it if you die.*

K'aia leaned into the comforting touch. *We're there for each other; that's how it works. I had to have the enhancement, so let's make me the most indestructible Yollin there's ever been.*

Alexis gave K'aia a knowing look. *I totally just saw you thinking about Kael-ven.*

K'aia cracked her neck and dropped into a half-stance. *Yeah, let's see his old ass ignore me when I can kick it from one side of the* G'laxix Sphaea *to the other.* She shadowboxed to emphasize her point. *See if he still calls me "child" then.*

Trey gagged. *Wouldn't his grandson be more your age?*

The Yollin tilted her head and threw a dirty look Trey's way. *Oh, I got over that after speaking to him. He's a great warrior, but I didn't find him to be the most interesting conversationalist.*

You expected differently? Trey lifted a finger when the comprehension train hit him at full speed. *Never meet your heroes.* Now *the saying makes sense.*

Alexis raised an eyebrow. *It didn't already?*

Trey looked at Alexis like she was a Coke short of a six-pack. *No? I met my hero, and she turned out to be the freaking Empress in disguise. How could I be disappointed by that?*

Trey got ahead of Alexis and K'aia and took a seat on the bench next to Gabriel as Alexis and K'aia headed for an empty space farther back. He bumped Gabriel with an elbow. "What's with the serious look?"

Gabriel's attention was on the NPCs. He and Alexis were the only humans, but the non-player characters were mostly familiar species. They hadn't spent much time with any of them except Sibil and Gorrak. "We're soldiers now. These are the people we'll depend on, and they should be able to depend on us, too. I think we should have done more to bond with our unit. Then we wouldn't be headed into the next part of the game with fourteen strangers at our backs."

Trey grinned. "There's only one way to remedy that." He offered a hand to the lump of living granite opposite. "Good to meet you. The name's Trey. I'm a Baka, the human is Gabriel."

"Boden, I'm a Chrlič," he replied in a voice like grinding pebbles. He clasped Trey's hand, then Gabriel's. "Good to meet you. You two are the only ones from your unit?"

Gabriel hitched a thumb to the other end of the transport, where Alexis and K'aia were strapped in with Sibil and Gorrak on either side of them. "My sister, Alexis. The Yollin is K'aia, Sibil is the…" He paused and smiled. "You know, I'm not sure what Sibil is. I never asked her. Gorrak is the Shrillexian."

Alexis waved. *You came to the same conclusion as me, then?*

These guys are pretty fun! She flashed Gabriel a bright grin before returning to the conversation.

Boden inclined his head in return. "Your unit did well. Only Slash and me made it through from ours."

The Noel-ni named Slash peered out from a shock of dark facial fur and jerked her chin in greeting. "'Sup?"

"That's nothing," a Leath a few seats down scoffed. "I had to transfer because I outlasted everyone in my unit. You're looking at the sole survivor of *both* those units."

"Let me guess," Trey called. "Interrogation wiped your second unit out?"

The Leath nodded, a stark expression replacing his easy grin of a moment ago. "That was brutal. Jentek, by the way."

The introductions went on as the transport lifted off and continued until the doors opened on an enormous hangar.

The Yollin SI got to his two feet and held the team back from the rush for the exit with a hand. "Before you go, I wanted to thank you six on behalf of all the SIs for exposing the truth about the corruption at the Corral."

Alexis smiled. "It was the right thing to do." Her smile faded momentarily. "Sorry, Staff. I don't know your name."

The SI smiled. "Torrence." He shook his head to dismiss the team's humble mumblings. "Listen up. You weren't at the Corral to do the right thing. You were there to learn how to obey orders. What you did took courage, even if you went about it like a bunch of school kids. Speaking up when you see injustice is hard. We're all grateful to see the backs of those bullying jerkholes."

He glanced at the other corporals with a rueful smile.

"Zenith Station is tough. Most of you won't last six months. I was deployed there for just over six years before I realized my path lay with teaching. If you need anything while you're there, Commander Childers is the person to ask if you can't find me. I'll put in a good word for you all when we get out of stasis."

Trey thought he'd misheard. "Did you just say you're going with us to Zenith Station?"

Torrence nodded, the medals on the breast of his uniform bobbing in rhythm with his speech. "Normally I'd hand you over officially here and return to the Corral, but I requested a transfer so I could keep my eye on your group."

Gabriel thanked him. "I know we're going to appreciate that."

Torrence ushered them onto the ramp, moving ahead of them as he spoke. "You won't appreciate a thing if you get stuck out of stasis for the next eight months. Get a move on, soldiers."

They all thanked Torrence again as they exited the transport.

"Where to now?" Trey asked, glancing nervously at the stasis Pods set out in rows with six feet of space between them.

Alexis flicked her gaze toward the pair of medical technicians standing by two chairs.

"I'm gonna guess the line for the people in white coats isn't going to end with a lollipop," K'aia snarked. "For a Yollin who isn't keen on doctors, I've met an awful lot of them recently."

Sibil poked her head out of the line. "K'aia?" She

grinned. "Hey! Where did you guys get to? Gorrak had me convinced you'd been cut at the last second."

"Still here," Gabriel assured her. "K'aia gets a little nervous when it comes to doctors."

Sibil pulled Gorrak out of the line by the sleeve, and the two of them walked to the back to join the others. "What do you make of the other corporals?"

Gorrak made his opinion clear with a look.

Sibil dismissed it with a hiss. "I know what grumpy-pants here thinks. He didn't say a word to anybody but Alexis and me all the way here."

K'aia fixed him with a fond look. "You can do better than that. You got to know *us*. That didn't work out so badly, did it?"

Gorrak's glare softened at the warmth in K'aia's reasonable tone. "I haven't made up my mind yet."

They reached the technicians and received an injection before being shown to their stasis Pods.

See you on the other side, Alexis told the others. A thrill went down her spine as the lid closed. *I have a good feeling about this.*

CHAPTER TWO

Zenith Station

Alexis woke feeling like six pounds of hamburger in a five-pound bag. She blinked as the fog cleared, and her mind came back into focus.

What was different? Her uniform felt restrictive for a start. She looked down at her chest and saw the reason her clothing was so tight. "Damn. *Those* sure grew!"

Unexpectedly enhanced breasts aside, her boots were also pinching, and her sleeves and trouser legs now ended above her wrists and ankles.

Alexis shook her much-longer hair out of her face and waited for the stasis Pod to open before rushing out on legs that wobbled for the first few steps. She felt similar confusion coming from Gabriel and K'aia. *You both okay? Trey? You're quiet.*

Yeah, K'aia answered as the Pod's lid opened to let her out. *Just... I wasn't expecting to* grow *any.* She walked out of the stasis Pod and tested each joint of her body gingerly. "I don't believe it. I'm perfect."

"I have a beard." Gabriel's four-word reply brought giggles from Alexis. He stepped over the lip of the Pod and stared at his sister. "What's so funny?"

"I don't even know where to begin," Alexis told him as she shucked her tight boots.

"How about with you looking like a younger, pirate version of your father?" Trey laughed, his amusement spilling over. "Alexis, you look just like your mother."

Alexis snickered. "It's true, you look like someone beefed Dad up in character creation." She wagged a finger at him. "Stop smiling! You're ruining the illusion."

Gabriel waved at Alexis. "Do the eyebrow thing, go on."

Alexis raised her eyebrow, then dissolved into giggles at the reaction she got from the others.

Not everybody was having the same easy transition from being in stasis. SI Torrence was working his way around the hangar with a group of technicians to remedy the situation. He left one or two of the white-coated medical specialists with each soldier, starting with the ones who had vomited upon waking.

Trey stretched his eight-and-a-half-foot frame and started working his muscles to test them. "This is the best! I have to be the biggest Baka since Qu'Hi. I wonder if people on Earth would mistake me for him?"

"Qu'Hi never went to Earth," Alexis refuted, rolling her eyes as she braided her hair. "You put two and two together and came up with the square root of pi after we watched *Star Wars*. There has to be a more reasonable explanation as to how George Lucas came up with the Wookiees than 'my ancestor visited Earth.'"

Trey lifted his hands in an approximation of a scale.

"On the one hand, we have Chewbacca, hairy alien warrior who sounds a heck of a lot like my Uncle Li'Orin after a heavy meal. On the other we have, Qu'Hi, a legendary Baka whose travel memoirs mention hairless apes on a blue planet. Sounds pretty likely to me." He smirked, loving how easy it was to rile Alexis up. "Can you prove my theory isn't real?"

Alexis snorted. "Can you prove it is? Statistically, the chances of yet another alien species are..." Her voice trailed off as she did the mental math. "Dammit."

Trey threw his hands up. "The proof is the whole part of human culture which celebrates him. Qu'Hi's legend is told on many worlds."

Gabriel chuckled. "Do the chances go up with each new alien who landed on Earth? There were a fair few, sis."

Alexis narrowed her eyes at her brother. "That's still not proof it happened." She pulled at her shirt. "I need a change of clothes. If I was wearing an atmosuit, it wouldn't be a problem."

SI Torrence finished tending to Boden, then walked over to the group with his technicians in tow. "How are you all adjusting? Any signs of stasis sickness?"

Alexis gave up on the boots she was wearing. "I don't think so. A uniform that fits wouldn't go amiss. I'm also shoeless."

Torrence nodded. "Good. The techs are going to take your vitals and check your reactions, then you can make your way through the doors over there to get seats for orientation."

He left them with three technicians, who performed the same observations as the technicians at the Corral had—

minus the injection—before handing them each a pair of dog tags, and releasing them with instructions to go straight to orientation.

They made their way through the doors and into the auditorium beyond.

Trey paused when he saw the group they'd traveled with was spread out around the auditorium. "Where do we sit?"

Alexis pointed to a line of empty seats in the front row. "Down there."

"The back," Gabriel decided simultaneously.

"Middle it is," Trey concluded. "We haven't got all day to discuss the pros and cons of seat choice."

K'aia laughed as she spied the Yollin-adapted seat. "Keep talking sense, and I'm going to start thinking maybe Eve gave you a dose of maturity along with the nanocytes."

Trey sidestepped into the narrow space between their row and the one behind to let the others go first, doing his best to insert his bulk. "It's more to do with the armed officers on the stage looking at us as though they're wondering if we're going to be trouble."

"Don't make eye contact," Sibil advised. She hopped over K'aia's intended seat and slid into the chair between that and Gabriel's, and Trey and K'aia took their seats.

Gorrak indicated the lack of space with a frustrated wave. "Where am I supposed to sit?"

Sibil pointed Gorrak at the row of seats in front of her. "Consider it a chance to get to know some of our teammates."

Slash and Boden turned when they heard Sibil's voice.

Boden patted the empty seat beside him with a heavy hand. "We don't bite.

Jentek grunted. "Well, *I* don't. Can't speak for Slash."

"What kind of name is 'Slash' for a Noel-ni?" Trey wondered aloud.

Slash was suddenly standing in Trey's lap with one hand around his throat and the other pulled back for a strike.

"You wanna find out?" Slash inquired sweetly. She looked over her shoulder, finding her wrist caught in Gabriel's hand. "Let go of me!"

Gabriel shook his head. "Not happening, fluffball. You don't threaten my friend and get away with it."

Trey's eyes widened in awe at the razor tips on Slash's splayed claws. "Cool! Guess I know how you got your name." Momentary confusion marred his usually sunny features. "But...are they a permanent modification? 'Cuz I don't like your chances when you have an itchy ass if they are."

Slash released Trey and laughed as she climbed back to her own seat. "Wouldn't you like to know?" Gorrak sat beside Boden, casting a doubtful look at the Noel-ni.

Alexis relaxed when the Noel-ni proved to be no more immune to Trey's innocent charm than the rest of them. She cast her gaze over the auditorium, taking a quick estimate of the number of people in the room. She counted almost a hundred people, all dressed in the same plain black uniform, before her effort was cut short by the arrival of their new commanding officers.

A male Ixtali bearing a general's insignia swooped in through the doors, followed by his retinue of staff. He mounted the stage without pausing to break the silence that had fallen with his entry.

The team recognized the similarity to the way General Kispin's staff had operated. The Ixtali's entourage fanned out and took their various positions with an air of calm efficiency.

Trey wrinkled his nose at the sheer girth of the Shrillexian staff sergeant's neck as he squeezed into the chair behind the table set out for him on the stage. "I'd think we were gonna miss Sergeant Lokkel's tender loving care," he whispered. "But we might get more nurturing from this slab of angry muscle than we ever did from the ice queen."

He settled in his seat when the lights shifted and flooded the stage.

The general took his position in the center of the stage and gazed out unblinkingly. "I am Commander Ixtayne. Welcome to Zenith Squadron, candidates. You were the best and brightest of your intake groups during basic training, the favored few who convinced your base commanders that you have the potential to claim a place with the best of the best. Some of you might even have been told that you are 'special.'

"Those halcyon days are over. Here is the reality check that will save your lives many times in the months to come." He shifted the hem of his robe and took a step closer to the edge of the stage.

"You are the *least* qualified assets aboard this station. Every person here outranks you in both knowledge and experience. Remembering that will serve to keep you alive long enough to pass the course."

A murmur of concern rippled through the seated soldiers.

Commander Ixtayne paused to let the information sink in, his inner calm shown by his inactive mandibles. "Do not fear. Your basic training has prepared you for the rigors of the course. Over the next weeks, you will become acquainted with the station and the syllabus. Mandatory physical testing will begin in two days and will be repeated every four weeks. After that, candidates will be placed into units for the duration of training."

The commander turned his upper body to the Shrillexian and held out an expectant hand. "The list if you please, Grom."

The staff sergeant handed him a datapad with a respectful nod.

"Thank you. The Zenith course is intended to provide candidates the critical knowledge and skill base needed to perform the duties of an officer in an unconventional warfare situation." Commander Ixtayne took a moment to scroll down the tablet he'd been offered. He read out the course requirements, stating which modules were mandatory as he went. "While the focus of the course is problem analysis and resolution, and modules offering language, medical, and interpersonal skills are not required, we will look more favorably upon candidates who have shown initiative, come selection time."

Gabriel pondered the ratio of study to practical exercises. *I'm getting the impression we're going to be spending a lot of time in the classroom.*

Alexis liked the sound of that. *I'm glad. This is our chance to figure out where our place is in the real world.*

What do you mean? Trey asked.

Alexis pursed her lips as she considered. *We came into this gameworld to learn how to lead, right? Our goals have changed. We don't need to lead anyone if we can do our part to bring the Seven to Justice. It's not like we haven't already fought every day of our lives in one way or another.*

"Victorious warriors win first and then go to war, while defeated warriors go to war first and then seek to win," Trey quoted.

"The supreme art of war is to subdue the enemy without fighting," Alexis countered. *You have to do better than that if you're going to quote my own species' philosophers at me. If we want to be the best in the field, we have to pay attention in class. K'aia, you were annoyed when Kael-ven treated you like a child, right?*

K'aia nodded. *Well, yeah. I'm not a child. I've worked like Baba Yaga was driving me to be the best at what I do. What does that have to do with all these classes we have to take?*

Alexis tilted her head to concentrate on the commander as well as the conversation. *We are children, at least to people who have been around for hundreds of years. They've lived through everything we're going to learn here.*

Makes sense, Trey agreed. *Inexperience is the obstacle we have to overcome if we want to be taken seriously.*

Gabriel recalled a moment when General Kispin had reminded him of the real general in their lives, his grandfather Lance. *You're right.*

Commander Ixtayne got to the end of the list. "There is no need for me to go into detail. Suffice it to say that those who apply themselves to achieving excellence will be rewarded for their efforts. At the end of the course, the remaining candidates will participate in a live exercise, where everything you learned in training will be put into practice. Any soldier with extraordinary abilities will also be required to pass regular proficiency exams in their specialty."

He handed the datapad back to the staff sergeant. "If, and only if, you make it through this, you will be promoted to specialist. Right now, you will leave this room in an orderly manner and proceed at the direction of the staff instructors. Dismissed."

With that, the commander left the auditorium. The SIs spread out to monitor two rows each and started the task of organizing the candidates into a line at the doors at the rear of the room.

Gabriel spotted SI Torrence making his way toward them.

The Yollin waved the two rows of ten out when their turn to join the line came around. "Follow the candidate in front of you," he told K'aia. "First stop will be Supply."

Yay for footwear, Alexis enthused.

K'aia nodded and led the team out of the auditorium and into a utilitarian gray corridor. They walked at double-time to keep up until the line suddenly ground to a halt somewhere up ahead.

CHAPTER THREE

Zenith Station, Candidate Quarters

The seemingly endless lining up was over at last, and the team and thirty-four others, including Boden and Slash, had been deposited at the door to their quarters with the instruction to unpack everything they'd been given in Supply and prepare for the first round of testing.

Alexis made up her bunk, her mind on the feeling she had of being turned inside out and shaken into an entirely new shape, now she had a moment of quiet. Everything was different, not just her body. She hadn't noticed it right away, but her perspective had changed since Addix's death and their reinsertion into the game.

The recruitment methods of this military still bothered her, no matter that the majority turned out to be glad of the intervention. Perhaps she would feel better if the conscription was lawful, perhaps not. The game was just that to her now—a step out of time.

The time she and Gabriel had been kidnapped was front and center of her thoughts. Addix had made it out of that situation unscathed, which was more than could be said for the kidnappers.

Alexis realized that despite the wisdom her parents had shared, all that really mattered to her was getting through and out, so she could start getting revenge. Her heart hurt in the place Addix's memory resided.

She had *known* that people died. She and Gabriel had seen it happen both in and out of the gameworld. She hadn't understood that the inability to reach the lost person again was the true consequence of death.

What she was stuck on was how Addix had lived every day knowing she might be killed while protecting her and Gabriel. That she had survived their young childhood, only to give her life to save Trey's mother and the Bakas they'd been rescuing, felt unfair to Alexis.

Perhaps she would feel better about it if there had been something she could *do*. Mahi' had chosen to refuse the Pod-doc, saying she would bear the loss of her leg as a reminder to her people of the sacrifice made to ensure her survival.

That was the Baka way.

Alexis knew the way *she* could best honor her aunt's memory was to be the person she had seen in Addix's eyes. Even baddies had people who loved them—mothers, spouses, children. Was it fair to take from them because their loved one messed up?

That's why prisons were invented, Gabriel interrupted softly, hearing the tumultuous thoughts turning in his sister's mind.

Alexis looked across at his bunk. *I'm not thinking of crim-inals. Crime has its own set of issues and solutions. We accepted this scenario, but we know that most of the soldiers are conscripts.* She sighed and said aloud, "I'm thinking about war."

"What about war?" Gorrak asked, perking up at the mention of his new favorite subject.

Alexis wrinkled her nose in thought as she settled into a cross-legged position. "How do we know we're fighting on the right side?"

"How does anyone know?" Gorrak retorted. "We're just cogs in the machine. Let the higher-ups go to the trouble of thinking."

"Listen to Bullet Bait," a mocking voice intruded. The female Torcellan the voice belonged to sneered at the team.

"Linda, be careful!" one the Torcellan's two friends spluttered. "They're with humans!"

Linda scoffed at the two males. "What do I care? Humans aren't the shit. They will all be buried together when that dumb Shrillexian messes up. How did he even get through basic?"

Sibil launched herself over the rail of her bunk and flew at the bitchy Torcellan. "I'll bury you, you speciesist!"

K'aia plucked Sibil out of the air before she could tear into Linda with her claws. "Don't fall for it," she told the apoplectic reptilian. "She's too weak to make it, so she's trying to get rid of the competition. Starting a fight is a sure way to get cut from the program."

Sibil shook free of K'aia's grip. "Fine," she acquiesced with a grumble. "But I'm going to whip her sorry ass come training." She threw Linda and her group a dirty look. "It must suck to know the only way to win is to cheat."

Linda opened her mouth but had no comeback. She

grunted in annoyance and flounced off toward the other side of the room with her clique in tow.

Alexis met Gabriel's dark gaze and saw that the altercation had riled him. "You okay?"

Gabriel shrugged and went back to making his bunk. "Anyone who isn't going to work for the good of us all is going to fail the course. Like K'aia said," he told her, "she's not worth our effort."

Zenith Station, Training Facility, Testing Labs

SI Torrence ushered the candidates through the swinging doors. He paused in the atrium beyond, which led to five doors separated by plexiglass windows. "Welcome to testing. Every Zenith candidate goes through a series of mental and physical challenges designed to give the selection committee a picture of your progress."

Trey raised his hand. "What does the selection committee do?" he asked after Torrence nodded permission to speak.

"They meet each month to decide which candidates get cut from the program." Torrence waved down the reaction from the candidates. "You all knew this wasn't going to be as simple as showing up. The committee will be looking for the candidates with the highest levels of improvement to advance. Those with the lowest margins will be cut. Today's session is all about giving us a baseline to work with. Do your best."

Gabriel picked up a whisper at the back of the group. He tuned out the explanation Torrence was giving them about the various testing rooms to listen in on Linda ordering the two male Torcellans around as though she owned them.

Alexis caught Gabriel's distracted gaze and figured he was listening to the Torcellans. She tugged his sleeve to bring him back to the instructions at hand. *We can take care of her later,* she told him. *We have to keep our heads in the game.*

I'm concerned for those guys, Gabriel admitted. *Did you hear how she speaks to them? She's threatening to have their families harmed if they don't help her get through. I can't see why they have to listen to that poison.*

It's how Torcellan society works, Alexis reminded him. *She outranks them just by being female. They're going to jump to do her bidding no matter how vile she is in the hope she'll choose one of them for a marriage contract.*

K'aia was no more impressed than the others. She made her way to the twins when the group broke up to head to the first room they'd been assigned. *It's just unfortunate for those males that the female they're courting is a dictator without a pair of brain cells to rub together.*

Alexis didn't disagree. *The process will weed her out,* she told them. *If you were listening to Torrence, you would have heard that we're going to be tested individually. She can't cheat even if she tries.*

She took her seat at one of the computer stations and opened her holoscreen by pressing her hand to the reader embedded in the desk.

"Welcome, Candidate Nacht, A," a soft female voice intoned.

Alexis smiled and gestured at her screen to prove her

point. "See? Linda can be as bossy as she likes. She can't have the guys take the test for her."

Linda shot Alexis a dirty look, which Alexis repaid with a bright smile that only annoyed the Torcellan more.

Trey slid into the chair at the station beside hers and activated his computer. "This is kind of intimidating," he admitted.

A candidate resembling a small dog spoke up. "What are we being tested on? I'm more in favor of physical challenges."

Slash and Boden agreed.

Sibil took her seat with a nervous smile. "It can't be that bad, right?"

Gorrak could only stare at the screen, perplexed. "I just hope I can read the questions," he fretted.

Torrence overheard the candidates' nervous remarks. He made his way to the front of the room and raised his hands for quiet. "It's okay to feel daunted if you haven't been in an exam situation before. Just relax, and you'll be fine. The test is designed to work to your ability and improve your knowledge as well as track your progress with each session. Every candidate begins with the same questions. There are no right or wrong answers. The system will adapt to your ability."

Except there are, Alexis countered, looking at the user interface. *I've taken some of the adaptive learning modules ADAM designed for the military back when Mom had the empire.*

Of course, you have, Gabriel teased.

Alexis shot him a stern look. *Do you want to know what I know or not?*

26

It was too late for her to share, anyway. Torrence dimmed the lights and instructed them to begin the program.

Gorrak was given a headset to counter his illiteracy, with the assurance from Torrance that there was no shame in not having had the opportunity to learn. The next two hours went by at varying speeds for the candidates. The silence was broken occasionally by a groan of frustration from someone who was stumped, sometimes followed by Torrence's soft voice talking the candidate through the meaning of the question they were stuck on.

Alexis worked in complete silence as the system guided her at speed through questions designed to test her reactions to various situations she might encounter while on duty, interspersed with mathematical problems, logic problems, and a host of others she was interested in finding out the purpose of.

To be asked how she would deal with looters on a warring planet was one thing. To be asked what she would take if *she* was the looter threw her enough that she almost missed the next question entirely. She figured her ethics were being tested as well as her logic skills, which she hoped meant their commanding officers were looking for the candidates who would make the right choices in sticky situations.

Gabriel blocked the barrage of thoughts from Alexis while he concentrated on answering his questions. His was not to reason why. He just wanted to make it through this and get to the physical part of the testing process. Still, he gave the questions his full attention.

He looked up when Alexis left her station.

I'm finished, she told him. *The instruction is to go to the next room and wait for the next test to begin.*

Gabriel glanced at his progress bar and saw he was eighty percent complete on his test. *Looks like I'm almost done. Tell me what you see in the next room.*

He continued to work through his test while Alexis gave him a heads-up on the situation in the next room.

There are a bunch of technicians, she informed him, opening the link to K'aia and Trey at the same time. *Different apparatus that I can't tell the function of. I want to say it's torture equipment, but if I'm being reasonable, it's probably for exercise. There are ballistics dummies. They have one side of the room sectioned into, well, sort of cubicles is the only way I can describe them. The techs manning those look pretty nervous.*

Gabriel grinned. *It sounds like we're going to be put through our paces with our extra abilities.*

Alexis sat against the wall, closed her eyes, and opened the e-reader in her internal HUD. She was very used to being first to finish in class, and she was a good way into her study of the Kurtherian technology her parents had brought back from Qu'Baka, thanks to Eve's updates.

It was a good distraction from the anger that reared its head whenever she allowed her mind to run free.

CHAPTER FOUR

Alexis continued to read until she was joined by the next candidate to finish, the canid who had joined the conversation earlier.

"You're either a pretty smart human, or you didn't pay attention to what you were clicking," she told Alexis as greeting.

Alexis smiled upon seeing the humor lighting her eyes. "You too." She got to her feet and offered her hand. "I'm Alexis."

"Pootie," she replied, looking at Alexis' hand with curiosity.

Pootie - By Eric Quigley

"It's a human custom," Alexis explained. "We shake to show we're friendly."

Pootie tilted her head and placed a paw out for Alexis to complete the exchange. "Interesting. We don't get many humans on my planet." She retrieved her paw and fished around in a pocket of her embroidered robe. "We exchange gifts on Leia. Here."

Alexis accepted the small, plastic-wrapped block with a smile. "Thank you." She frowned lightly at the pungent smell. "What is it?"

"Plastique," Pootie told her in the same tone Alexis might have used to describe children's toy putty. "It's a special blend I came up with that has more bang for the same stability."

Alexis stored the gift carefully, even though she was aware that plastic explosives were normally stable until detonated. "You're an explosives fan, huh? Let me see what I can give you in return." She did a quick search through the data stored in her HUD and located a theory William had come up with regarding the modification of traditional explosives for use in non-standard environments. "I think you'll get a kick out of this."

She transmitted it to the Leian's datachip upon instruction. Pootie's eyes lit up as she skimmed the first page. "You're right. This is interesting!" She grasped Alexis' hand again. "Well met, Alexis. You can count on me to have your back."

The door swung open to admit Linda and her entourage. The three of them swept past Alexis and Pootie with their noses in the air.

"Stuck up as a feline," Pootie remarked about Linda. "I can't understand how people like her get through life so easily."

Alexis shrugged. "Because others allow it."

Pootie wrinkled her nose. "Not me."

"No," Gabriel agreed as he entered the room and joined them. "Me, either."

Alexis had her eyes on the two males whose names they didn't know. "I can't stand how they bow to her. I know they have their cultural thing going on, but nobody should feel like they have to obey the whims of a bully. I wonder…"

The door opened again to admit K'aia, Trey, Sibil, and

Slash, distracting Alexis from her thoughts of freeing the males from Linda's grip.

The rest of their unit filtered in over the next few minutes, minus a few stragglers who were taking longer with the test.

The head technician waved the group over to the cubicles. "Welcome, candidates. I am Specialist Pawson, and this is where you will be tested physically so that we can discover your limits, then work to extend them. First things first. We're going to get you wired up to the tracking system. My techs are going to place these pads on the relevant parts of your bodies. When your turn comes, strip to the waist if you're wearing clothing so they can put the pads around your heart."

Gabriel touched Alexis' mind while he was being fitted with sticky pads by the technician. *Are you still thinking about Linda?*

Yeah, she admitted. *I shouldn't be this distracted, but it's bothering the hell out of me, seeing those poor males get treated that way.*

They chose it, Gabriel reminded her. *That's free will, no matter how much it rubs us up the wrong way.*

The technician, a female Noel-ni, smiled at Alexis. "Lift your arm for me."

Alexis did so, and the pads were placed next to her heart. She gasped at the chill of the adhesive.

"Cold, right?" the technician sympathized. "Don't worry. They'll be at body temperature in two shakes of a canid's tail."

"Hey!" Pootie complained from the next cubicle. "Fewer

of the canid jokes. It's bad enough I'm going to be cleaning this glue out of my fur forever."

"It could be worse," Trey called. "They're not shaving us."

"That could easily be arranged," the technician murmured to Alexis with a wink. She held out two more pads. "These are the last ones. Move your hair, please."

Alexis snickered as she pulled her hair away from her temple to receive the pads. "Don't give him ideas," she told the Noel-ni in a conspiratorial whisper.

Alexis rejoined the group once she'd dressed again. She took one look at Trey's disarranged fur and dissolved into a giggle. "You look like you stuck your finger in a power outlet."

Trey pointed at Alexis. "You put your shirt on inside out."

Alexis looked down and saw that she had. She darted back into the cubicle and fixed it.

"This is where we split you up," Specialist Pawson told them as Alexis rejoined the group. "I have both Nachts down as having skills with energy manipulation. You two will be working separately from the rest of the unit once you've completed the physical testing." She pointed out the section of the room that was split into closed cubicles. "Those are the null chambers. You will be supervised by a specialist at all times."

The twins glanced at the technician waiting for them.

What do you think? Gabriel asked.

Alexis shrugged. *Too early to tell.*

Gabriel returned to listening mode as Specialist Pawson continued her introductions to the various stations around the room and the technicians running them.

Alexis automatically gravitated toward Gabriel, K'aia, and Trey. They stepped onto the treadmills at the first station and put on the masks the Zhyn technician pointed out.

"These are to measure your respiratory function," he told them as the treadmills started. "You will run."

Trey caught Gabriel's eye as the technician turned to his monitor. *Chatty guy.*

Gabriel suppressed a chuckle. *I know, right?*

The task took up the next hour while the technician ran the group through programs of increasing resistance and speed. The day passed in a whirlwind of being hooked up to the equipment at each station while the technicians measured their physical capabilities.

They broke when a Yollin wearing a catering staff uniform brought in a covered antigrav cart.

"Chow time," Specialist Pawson announced. "You have thirty minutes."

"Looks like we're going to be here a while longer," K'aia murmured so only the twins and Trey could hear.

Trey wiped the wet fur from his eyes, wishing he'd thought to tie it back before the sweat-fest had begun. "Here's hoping that's real food and not mush."

His plea was answered when they got to the head of the line. Each received a hotpack and a napkin-wrapped eating utensil, which they took over to a clear space by the wall. They sat in a circle on the floor to eat.

"It's looking good so far," Gabriel ventured hopefully. He pressed his thumbs to the indents to activate the hotpack and gave it a few seconds before peeling back the lid.

Alexis breathed a sigh of relief when she did the same and the solid food inside was revealed. "I don't care what planet this food is from. I'm just glad we get to chew it." She took a moment to decide between the meat, the veggies, and the grain that looked like fluffy rice, then dug into the veggies. "Mmmm."

Trey made small sounds of satisfaction as he chewed his meat. "Flavor," he enthused between bites. "No more holding my nose while I eat."

The enthusiasm wasn't limited to their group. All too soon, the meal was over, and Specialist Pawson called for a return to testing.

She sent Gabriel and Alexis to the null chambers, where the smiling technician from earlier awaited them.

"What do we do in there?" Alexis asked, eyeing the empty room beyond the clear wall with skepticism.

The technician took her feet down from where she'd been resting them on her workstation and pressed a button to open the chambers. "You're going to cut loose. We want to know how much energy you're capable of pulling from the Etheric, and what ways you can manipulate it. Sound good?"

Gabriel wasn't so sure it was a good idea for him to let that amount of energy run free, never mind what Alexis could do. "Um, not really. We could destroy the whole station if we aren't careful."

"Not really," the technician told them. "The chambers are designed to absorb and safely channel any energy that's expended inside them. Go on in. You're going to feel a pull on your energy once the chamber is activated, and that's just fine. I want you to take a minute to acclimate to the sensation of being 'drawn on' before we get started."

The twins exchanged hesitant glances before they entered their respective chambers.

I suppose we're just going to reset if we blow this place to pieces, Alexis conceded.

Gabriel rolled his eyes. *Yeah, and that's not going to hurt at all.*

The doors closed, cutting them off from the rest of the testing lab.

"Can you still hear me?" Alexis asked, feeling a chill as the chamber was activated.

"Loud and clear," Gabriel assured her.

There was a crackle, and the voice of their technician came from a hidden speaker. "Okay, let's get started. See the dark panel at the back of the chamber?"

The twins replied that they did.

"I want you to do your best to break it," she instructed. "Take it easy at first, or the chamber will drain your energy faster than you can pull it."

Alexis looked at Gabriel and shrugged as she opened a link to the Etheric and manifested a ball of flame over each hand. "You've got it." She aimed at the panel and sent the burning energy at it with force. Contrary to what her mind had told her would happen, the stream of Etheric energy did not blow a hole in the chamber.

Gabriel observed for a moment before igniting his own flame. "So, what? We just keep increasing our output until we reach the chamber's tolerance?" he asked the technician.

"You'll find it pretty damn difficult to make a dent," she assured them. "These chambers were designed in the Etheric Empire by BMW and tested to destruction by the Empress. We knew you were coming and prepared accordingly."

The twins relaxed at hearing that their mother, even if it was the gameworld version, had been the one to idiot-proof the technology.

Alexis gradually increased her output, taking it slow while she got used to the feeling of her excess being siphoned off by whatever technology the chamber ran on.

Gabriel was glad he didn't feel like he had to hold back for once. "Check this out," he called, switching his flow to create pointed bars of solid energy.

Alexis glanced through the transparent wall and grinned. "Oh, you want to play? Watch *this*."

Zenith Station, Training Facility (twelve weeks later)

The candidates watched the holovid with varying degrees of fascination and horror.

Onscreen, a specialist unit advanced through an urban setting with their weapons raised. The civilians were armed and fought back as the specialists gassed the crowds, then bagged and tagged them individually for transport.

Many of the candidates watching had gone through a similar experience. They stared at the holoscreen as the specialists loaded the unconscious civilians into vehicles, too shocked to do anything except observe as the protesters were kidnapped.

SI Torrence laced his hands on his desk as the holovid

ended. "What you have just seen is the harsh reality of the recruitment process. As specialists, you will be called upon to carry out this duty wherever we find a planet within the enemy's reach."

He met the eyes of the candidates with a slow, sweeping gaze. "Make no mistake. We are doing these people a kindness. If this was how you were recruited, the world you once knew is gone.

"What do you mean, 'gone?'" Boden called.

Torrence shook his head. "The enemy's practice is to strip-mine the planets they come across for every resource, including the people. We can only save so many when we are met with hostility, and we can only protect those worlds that devote themselves fully to the war."

K'aia understood better than most in the room. "This way, whole civilizations aren't lost forever. The survivors are taken to the Corral or somewhere like it, and the species lives on."

"Exactly," Torrence agreed. "Since we are a military, we can provide for as many soldiers as we can take in. Allowing a species to go extinct on the basis of 'we don't want to be part of a war' isn't ethical, as we see it."

Alexis found her opinion on the conscription method shifting as the lecture went on. Right and wrong depended on the perspective of each party. The conscripts became soldiers, or they were reassigned to production work when they washed out of Basic. The ones who advanced were trusted with the truth—or part of it, at least—and sent out to increase the ranks of fighters keeping their still-nameless enemy at bay.

It made sense if you didn't take free will into account.

She wondered if those at the top considered them as anything except resources to be applied to their problem.

SI Torrence wrapped up his lecture with a final remark. "The next twelve weeks will be dedicated to ensuring you will survive when inserted into a hostile situation. Pay close attention to the specialists teaching you."

Gabriel remained in his seat after Torrence dismissed the class and waited until the room had cleared before approaching their instructor with his problem.

Torrence smiled, his mandibles parting in a more human than Yollin expression. "Gabriel, what's up?"

Gabriel leaned against the desk behind him and folded his arms. "I have a couple of questions about the video," he told him. "This isn't sitting right with me."

Torrence tilted his head in understanding. "You come from the Etheric Empire, right? So you know exactly why we use the system we have. We were not blessed with an Empress to inspire the masses to take up arms."

Gabriel nodded. "Yeah, I get that. The thing is, rolling up on some unsuspecting planet and forcing people to fight isn't just, or honorable, or any of the things I was brought up to be. What gives the leaders of this military the right to tell people how to live? To force them to fight?"

Torrence sighed as he placed a hand on Gabriel's shoulder. His tone and demeanor shifted to those of a confidant. "I don't make the rules. I just teach them. Look, I've been to the front line. The enemy..." His voice trailed off, his gaze becoming distant with harsh memories. "We might be curtailing the freedom of individuals, but in this circumstance, there's no other way to ensure they survive what's out there."

Gabriel didn't see how that was relevant to his unit being ordered to suppress revolutionary action on conscripted planets. "Surely there are enough volunteers to fight?"

Torrence chuckled softly. "You humans. Not every species is willing to pick up arms and fight for their people, much less any other race in need. I want you to take a look at the archives and learn the history of this galaxy."

Gabriel furrowed his brow. "How's that relevant?"

"History is vital," the SI explained. "If we do not look to the past, we are doomed to repeat the same mistakes over and over. I want you to read through the archives and get some understanding of why this model works."

"What about the enemy?" Gabriel ventured. "When will we learn about them?"

"Soon," SI Torrence promised with more than a little regret. "All too soon. Dismissed."

Alexis was waiting when Gabriel exited the classroom. "What was that about?" she asked.

Gabriel bumped her with his shoulder as they set off walking. "I'm with you on the conscription issue," he confessed. "Torrence told me to read through the archives to get some understanding. Apparently, we humans are quicker than the rest to defend what's right."

Alexis grinned. "That's the nicest way another species has described us since we've been here." She flipped her hair over her shoulder. "Personally, I think Torrence is right. It's not like they've got Mom here to inspire them. Can you imagine Linda rushing in to save anyone but her own?"

Gabriel wrinkled his nose in distaste. "I couldn't even

see her saving *them*, but then she's a selfish bitch who couldn't be relied on to piss on you if you were on fire."

"That's an insult to bitches and firefighters everywhere," Alexis countered. "But 'selfish' describes Linda's group perfectly. What's next on your schedule for today?"

Gabriel checked in his internal HUD and found the next class. "Oh, that's just great. Another brutal session with Specialist Childers."

Alexis grinned. "Oh, hells. Me too. Come on, we don't want to be late. He'll use us for target practice."

CHAPTER FIVE

They made it to the training center on the bottom deck just in time to fall in at the back of the line outside the doors as the Leath instructor arrived.

Late or not, Specialist Childers had a hard-on for punishing the candidates, and the two humans especially. He shook his head as the twenty candidates entered the vaulted room. "If it isn't my favorite class. Get a move on, candidates. We haven't got all day."

K'aia and Trey led the line as they filed in and took their usual places in a circle around the specialist.

Jentek grumbled as he took his position, "Curse the Seven and the burden they put upon my family. I never asked for this." He nodded at Gabriel and Alexis. "It's a damn shame the Empress didn't defeat them sooner. Maybe my family wouldn't have fled Leath, and I wouldn't be stuck in this class with the likelihood of getting my genitals blown off for looking at the instructor in the wrong way."

Alexis went for Jentek with her fist cocked, ready for a

fight. "I hate to be the one to tell you this, but your people only ever met one clan of the Seven. The Phraim-'Eh."

Slash leaned in and whispered out of the side of her mouth, "Maybe your people shouldn't have bought into Kurtherian lies in the first place. Power comes at a price, and those who have it don't share without taking their payment in blood."

Specialist Childers stopped Alexis before Gabriel had the chance to pull his sister back. The solid impact against the instructor's muscled arm sent Alexis stumbling back. "Your place, candidate, is to be quiet and obey. The Leath knew no better, and Jentek is not to blame for his affliction."

Jentek opened his mouth to agree but closed it again when he realized the specialist was insulting him as well as Alexis.

Alexis shot an apologetic look at Jentek and mouthed the word "Sorry." Specialist Childers was right. Jentek couldn't know that her mother had torn herself to pieces over the Leath war. It wasn't his fault, and it was wrong of her to jump down his throat just because she felt a certain way.

K'aia remained silent, as she always did in the training area. She saw little point in drawing attention to herself when their instructor took any opportunity to grind down their spirits. While she was aware that this pressure tactic was intended to bring the unit closer and force them to bond, she found it to be a test of her resolve to see the twins and Trey beaten and battered during Specialist Childers' close-combat lessons.

The SI took them through the warm-up before splitting

the candidates into five groups of four to begin the training exercise. "Today we will be putting into practice the urban infiltration techniques you have been studying for the last few weeks. Your goal is to pass through the city without being apprehended. This is a live exercise, so I don't want to see anyone playing out there."

Out where? Trey sent over the team channel. *What city?*

I'm sure we're going to find out, Alexis replied.

Specialist Childers indicated a door. "Through there is the airlock to your transport." His usually hard face softened. "Be aware of your surroundings at all times. I don't want to lose any of you to stupidity."

He joined the rear of the line and ushered the twenty candidates onto the transport. "Take your seats and strap in."

Slash and Boden joined Alexis, Gabriel, K'aia, and Trey on the right-hand bench.

"What is this?" Slash asked as the map came up in their helmet HUDs. "It looks like this city is already under Zenith control. Why send us there?"

Specialist Childers answered in a sharp tone, "It wouldn't behoove us to send untrained candidates into a hostile zone. However, do not take the exercise lightly. I can tell you that you will be up against various specialists who are scattered throughout the city. They will be armed with crowd-control equipment. Non-lethal, but I guarantee it will not be a pleasant experience if you are caught. Use what you have learned so far to avoid capture. There will be a reward for the teams who make it from the east wall to the west wall without being caught."

"What happens to the teams who don't make it?" Trey asked.

Specialist Childers shook his head. "Just don't fail."

The transport landed, and the unit spilled out into a dust storm.

Alexis was grateful for the protection her armor provided from the scouring wind. She turned up the heat in her armor and looked around for the others.

The other teams were forming tight huddles.

Gabriel grasped Alexis' hand and pressed a g-clip into her gauntlet. *Attach yourself to the rest of us,* he instructed. *This storm is likely to separate us if we're not smart about it.*

Alexis clipped the line to the attachment on the waist of her armor, and the team pressed close together to plan their entry to the city. *Okay, so we can't see the walls or even our hands in front of our faces. That means that the specialists can't see us either, not until we get close enough to be seen on infrared.*

Why doesn't this armor have stealth tech like ours? Trey asked. *I can't figure these menus out. I miss voice activation.*

You want your momma, too? Gabriel teased.

Trey smirked. *No, I want your mom. Then we could just walk through the city, and nobody would dare argue with us.*

Enough wishing for things that aren't going to happen, K'aia told them. *We need to move.* She took point, using the bulk of her body to shield the others from the wind as they crept closer to the city wall.

K'aia called a halt a few hundred meters from the base. *Would you look at that?*

What are we looking at? Trey complained. *I can't see in front of my visor.*

Look up, K'aia told him. *There's a welcoming party on the walls. Wait, I think I see Linda's team.*

They hung back while the other team approached.

It doesn't look like they know the specialists are up there, Alexis murmured. *Do you think we should tell them?*

Yeah, no, K'aia told her. She snorted as Linda's team was bombarded with suppression rounds by the specialists. *Couldn't have happened to a nicer set of assholes. But we should give the others a heads-up.* She opened a comm channel to Sibil. "You guys, there's a bunch of specialists manning the wall. Find another way in, and we'll meet up inside."

"Good to know," Sibil responded immediately. "Thanks, and good luck out there."

"You too," K'aia told her before dropping the connection. *It doesn't solve how we're going to get inside.*

Alexis pressed her lips together in thought. *Let me try something. We might be able to skip around the wall completely.* She opened a path into the Etheric. *It's going to be a push with our armor, but we can rest on the other side while we wait for Sibil and Gorrak.*

Gabriel sensed the parting of reality. *That's not large enough for K'aia to get through,* he told her. *Try adding my strength to yours.*

Alexis took his outstretched hand and immediately felt a surge in her ability to access the dimension. *Trey, you're first.*

Trey looked at Alexis' window in his HUD skeptically. *I don't know about that. What if you run out of juice and I get stuck there? Is the Etheric even the Etheric here?*

Alexis shrugged. *I have an open portal, so I'm guessing Eve was able to replicate it in some sense. Come on, I can't hold it all day.*

Trey turned a slow circle in the mists. "I have to say, I'm underwhelmed."

Alexis laughed along with the others. "What were you expecting?"

Trey shrugged. He was trying to spot any color besides gray. "I dunno. *Something*? This place is bland."

"That's because you're not connected to the energy," Gabriel explained. He waved a hand, and the mist around them reacted instantly. "See?"

Alexis narrowed her eyes and pressed her lips into a wicked smile as an idea occurred to her. "We don't need to go through the city at all."

K'aia knew that look. "What are you thinking?" she asked with more than a little wariness in her voice. "Because I'm pretty sure cutting through the Etheric wasn't an option Specialist Childers gave us."

Alexis held up a finger. "No, but Specialist Childers doesn't know we can access the Etheric, does he?"

Gabriel wrinkled his nose. "What about the training experience?" he countered. "It's all very well using our gifts to step outside the boundaries, but how does that help us learn anything new?"

Trey nodded. "Besides, I'm getting tired of just standing around. We need to get out of this place before we end up stuck in here."

Alexis caved. "Fair enough. I suppose you're right."

K'aia sighed in relief. "Then get us the hell out of here, so we don't get beaten by Linda's team."

Alexis held out her hands for them to take. "I doubt

Linda's team escaped the welcoming committee, but if you insist." She brought them out in a tree-filled park a few hundred meters inside the city wall.

K'aia grabbed the twins and pulled them into the cover of the trees when an explosion sounded nearby.

Gabriel caught Trey before he fell over a thick root protruding from the ground. "Easy, buddy."

Trey's eyes widened. "What's going on out there?"

Alexis peered out of the foliage. "It looks like Boden's team has made it through the wall, literally. There's a huge hole. Must have been Pootie."

"Nice!" Gabriel exclaimed in a low voice.

Trey scowled at the dust cloud beyond the park. "I only see Boden, Slash, and Jentek. Where's Pootie?"

They all peered out of the foliage to scan for the fourth member of the other team.

The Leian dashed out of the dust into the park, no less nimble for the heavy robes she wore in place of standard-issue armor.

Gabriel furrowed his brow as he considered the merits of having a munitions expert on hand. "What do you all think about joining up with them?"

"Nothing in the brief against working together," Alexis agreed. She opened a link to Sibil to give her and Gorrak their location. "I just called Sibil. That's got to be enough to make a winning team."

Trey cupped his hands around his mouth and called in a sharp whisper, "Pootie! Guys! This way!"

Pootie's keen hearing caught Trey's direction. She turned her canid-shaped snout into the wind and sniffed them out before ushering the rest of her team over to the stand of trees.

"Pootie sure took to the leadership role, huh?" Trey commented as she led her team across the park, hurrying them from one spot of cover to the next. "It's funny. She's half the size of Slash and twice as terrifying."

Gabriel chuckled. "Tell me about it. I thought she was a dog at first. Goes to show there are only so many models life forms into."

"Not true, Gabriel," Alexis pointed out. "Just because we've only 'discovered' carbon-based life forms, it doesn't mean that there aren't other life forms based on other elements."

Gabriel frowned. "I thought we were all carbon-based? I'm sure I remember Phyrro's lesson on that."

Alexis made a moue. "Yeah, no. You didn't take the advanced lesson where he went into all the other probabilities."

"This is no time for a science lesson," K'aia interrupted. "We're in the middle of a live exercise."

Trey grinned at Alexis' pouting. "I'm interested. Tell me about it when we get back to the station," he requested as the other teams arrived at their hiding place.

Pootie wasted no time getting down to business. "What do you know?"

Boden's quiet laughter had the sound of gently-shaken pebbles. "They know as much as we do," he told his erstwhile leader. "Calm down."

Pootie's face delivered the reply she was too polite to give verbally. "We're being graded on this exercise. I'm not playing here."

"Shame," Jentek commented, his eyes on the wall. "We could use some fun with all this seriousness."

Gabriel grinned as their friends arrived. "There will be time for fun after we win the exercise. You know Sibil and Gorrak, right?"

Alexis took a knee to be on eye level with Pootie and Slash, gesturing for the others to do the same. "Okay, everyone, get your maps up. If we work together, we can get to the endpoint without losing anyone."

Nobody had an argument for that. Pootie engaged her HUD, a transparent strip that came out of her headdress, while the others brought up their maps in their helmet HUDs.

Gabriel marked a number of places. "My best guess is that the specialists will be stationed at these points. Definitely here on the main road through the city center. Here, here, and here, at the transport links."

Trey nodded. "We should add the commercial quarter to the list."

K'aia nodded. "Yeah, and anywhere else that they can create a bottleneck."

Gabriel marked the shopping district as a no-go area.

Jentek's brow furrowed as he thought, which tightened the skin around his mouth enough so his tusks protruded. "What we need is a route the specialists won't expect anyone to take."

"What about underground?" Boden offered. "We could go through the sewer system."

Slash bared her teeth in disdain. "And spend the next month trying to get the stench of shit out of my fur? Are you crazy, stone man?" She ran a hand through her fur, one hand on her hip. "It's okay for you with your easy-wash bodies."

Trey patted Slash on the shoulder. "I appreciate the sentiment, but I'm pretty sure we're going to be getting worse things stuck in our fur once we go to war. Suck it up, buttercup."

"You're wearing armor," Alexis pointed out.

Boden made a face as he pointed at his shoulder joint. "You are lucky. You don't have crevices to clean out."

Slash tilted her head. "That's what you think."

Alexis wrinkled her nose. "Ew, TMI." She snickered at Slash's preening. "So, are we all agreed that the sewers are the way to go?"

Nobody had a good argument as to why not.

Alexis grinned and waved them on. "Then let's get moving before we run down the clock talking."

There was a hairy moment when they left the safety of the trees and ducked across the street to the nearest manhole.

K'aia and Boden hauled the heavy cover out of the way while the others kept watch on either end of the alley and the roofs of the surrounding buildings. Then they slipped into the darkness one by one.

Jentek dropped down last, his progress slowed by his effort to replace the manhole cover.

CHAPTER SIX

The Leath blinked while his helmet HUD adjusted for the darkness, then he cast his gaze around the pipe. "How come it's so big?" he asked. "When you suggested we came down this way, I expected to be crawling through on my hands and knees."

Alexis shook her head. "If we were in the suburbs, maybe, but this isn't even the main pipe for the city. It's probably going to get nasty once we hit the main sewer line, but we shouldn't have to crawl at any point."

"Amen to that," Trey put in, clasping his hands in gratitude. "But you can bet the specialists know that, too. We should be careful."

Gabriel double-checked that his air was being recirculated rather than drawn from outside his armor, glad for the barrier his helmet gave him against the stench of the sewage. "Agreed."

He looked around the pipe to check on the others. He felt bad for Pootie and Boden since the two of them weren't wearing armor.

K'aia was thinking the same. "Hey, Pootie. You wanna ride on my back?" She stuck a toe into the running water at their feet. "Don't want you drowning down here if it gets deep."

"That's pretty decent of you, K'aia," Pootie told her. She climbed up gratefully. "Next time, I won't refuse the armor."

Slash snorted. "Why does *she* get special treatment? What about me? I'm short, too."

Alexis raised an eyebrow, dropping her hands to her hips. "Seriously? Armor!"

K'aia chuckled as she indicated the spunky Noel-ni's full armor with a wave. "I'm pretty sure you'll be just fine."

She gave Boden a sympathetic smile. "Sorry you can't fit on my back as well."

Boden flashed a grin at K'aia. "I'll be fine. Nothing a good sandblasting won't fix once we get out of here." He folded his wings tightly around his body. "See? All good."

"Then we'd better get going," Alexis told the group. "Everyone ready?"

They moved down the pipe in a loose formation, keeping to silent communications in case they were wrong about the sewer system being beneath the specialists' notice.

Alexis kept the map up in her HUD to track their progress against the streets above their heads. They'd been walking for about an hour when they arrived at a nexus point where their pipe, along with eight others, fed into an even larger pipe.

The group came to a halt on the jutting ledge at the end

of the pipe where the water flowed over the edge into a churning river that half-filled the channel below.

Trey searched for the next part of their path and spotted the narrow walkways on either side of the river. "How do we get down there? It has to be a fifty-foot drop if one of us falls."

"Not to mention that current will sweep us right out of the city," Jentek added.

Boden spread his wings. "I can carry Pootie down there. Slash, too. The rest of you are too heavy for me to fly with."

Alexis got on her hands and knees. "Hold my feet," she told Gabriel.

Gabriel obliged, and Alexis inched out over the edge to get a look at the underside of the ledge.

"What do you see?" Trey asked.

"A ladder, I think," Alexis replied, pulling herself back onto the ledge. She shone her light on the grooves cut into the wall beside the ledge. "This side. No need to carry anyone, Boden."

Boden smiled. "Suit yourselves. I'll see you down there." He took off with a grace that belied his stocky frame.

Trey let out a low whistle of admiration.

"Shhh!" Slash hissed. "If there's anyone down here, they'll hear you!"

"I doubt they will," Trey refuted. "How are they going to pick anything up over the noise the water is making?"

Alexis rolled her eyes as she carefully hopped onto the ladder. "Because they'll have equipment. The same as us."

They descended in silence and continued heading deeper into the city.

Gabriel found his attention drifting with the monotony

of their surroundings after a few more miles of featureless pipe. Even the danger posed by the river faded to a dull roar after the first couple of times they were startled by a sewage drop from the feeder pipes above.

Alexis spoke up in his mind. *Do you think it's going to be this easy the whole way?*

Gabriel groaned internally. *I hope not. I might just die of boredom.*

Relief from possible death-by-boredom came in the form of a tight mesh gate blocking their way out of the main pipe.

The teams stood at the foot of the obstacle and searched its face for any clue as to how to open it.

"I think we've found the reason there were no specialists waiting down here," Trey commented unhelpfully.

K'aia grunted. "We've got an explosives expert with us, haven't we?" She looked around to locate the Leian member of their party. "Pootie, you're up."

"You don't have to ask me twice," Pootie told them amiably.

Pootie made her way to the gate with delicate steps and looked at it for a long moment. Then she dipped into her various pockets, bringing out and rejecting one plastic-wrapped package after another. Finally, she settled on the left inside pocket of her robe and brought out a package the size of a nut. "Make some room. In fact, you might want to back *riiiight* up. This stuff isn't for playing with."

They all did as instructed while Pootie shaved off a thumbnail's worth of the substance and stuck it on the metal grate. Then she returned to rummaging in her pockets. "Dang it. I'm out of det-cord."

Alexis manifested a spark of Etheric energy. "I can help with that."

Pootie looked at the spark uncertainly for a moment, then lifted a shoulder and walked over to join the rest of the group taking shelter behind one of the buttresses. "It should work. Go for it."

Alexis released the spark and sent it to ignite whatever explosive Pootie had stuck to the gate.

The resulting explosion shook the pipe, throwing the water up in a tidal wave and causing the team to be knocked off their feet.

Only K'aia remained standing. She picked Gabriel and Alexis up by their arms, then turned her attention to locating Trey.

Sibil and Gorrak let go of each other and called for Trey.

"I'm here," he replied, emerging dripping wet from farther back up the pipe. "But I can't see Pootie or Slash."

The Leian emerged from the recess of the buttress. "I'm fine."

Jentek was also unharmed. "Boden? He's gone, too. Are they lost?"

The Chrlič's wingbeats filled the pipe with an eerie whoosh. He flew over their heads and deposited a grumpy Slash on the ground before circling and making his landing. "I do not get lost. Our friend here was washed into the river and had to be rescued."

"Would have been fine," Slash grumped.

Alexis shook her head. "What would you have done? Swum up-current to get back to us?" She turned to Boden. "I'll thank you, even if she won't."

57

Gabriel was no happier with the Noel-ni's apparent ingratitude, but unlike his sister, he knew that it was more a case of bruised pride than anything for them to get offended about. He swept an arm toward the hole in the gate. "We have the ingress we needed, and we're all alive to joke about it. Let's go."

They climbed through the hole one at a time and paused briefly to check their maps before moving on.

Navigating the pipes was easy enough until they reached the end of the pipe, where it let out into the central processing plant.

Gabriel reached the mouth of the pipe first and called a halt, hearing voices despite the echoing thunder of water running through the many filtration tanks in the vaulted space beyond the pipe.

Trey got onto his stomach and cautiously peered over the edge of the walkway at the secondary tank below the main tank. "Specialists. Six of them."

"Well, we couldn't expect it to be empty the whole way," Sibil conceded. "What are we going to do?"

K'aia studied Trey's camera feed in her HUD. "They seem to be focusing on everywhere at once. It's not going to be easy to sneak past them."

Slash made her way to the front of the group. "I can get around out there without being seen."

Before anyone could stop her, Slash darted out of the pipe and leapt onto the rim of the main tank. She crawled along, aiming her helmet cam at the gantry midway up the tank to capture the specialists waiting there for the team.

"Are you getting this?" Slash whispered into her comm.

"Everything," Alexis confirmed.

Everyone examined the camera feed from Slash's helmet. The open floor between the tanks was set up to funnel any passersby into weapons range of the six specialists positioned on the gantry.

"I'm guessing they figured out we came down here," Trey remarked.

Gabriel furrowed his brow. "Come back around, Slash. Can we get to the other side?"

"Good question," Alexis murmured. "If we're lucky, they'll be expecting us to charge through and won't have prepared for any other eventuality."

Slash did as she was directed, moving slowly so she didn't draw the attention of the specialists. A few tense minutes later, her camera revealed a descending walkway leading from the rim of the main tank into a maze of filtration tanks. "Looks like we have our route."

K'aia saw a problem. "How do we get across to the tank without being seen?"

"We need a distraction," Pootie decided.

Alexis wrinkled her nose as she thought. "Do we?" She met the expectant stares of the others with a small smile. "Nothing in the rules said we can't engage."

"You want us to fight our way through?" Sibil exclaimed. "Didn't you learn *anything* from the last time we tried that?"

"Let's see them gas us down here," Gorrak countered, puffing out his chest.

Jentek chuckled as he put two and two together. "It was your unit who beat the crap out of the SIs at the Corral?" he asked. "I don't remember that going too well for you."

Gabriel nodded. "Yeah, but this is different. We're

supposed to do what's necessary to get to the endpoint. I'm with Alexis. Let's do this."

Trey got to his feet. "Alexis can take out the walkway. That will give us the chance to get across without the specialists catching us."

Alexis moved back from the edge. "We have to be careful not to cause them any injuries that can't be healed quickly. We don't know if they're due to be deployed after the exercise."

Gabriel nodded in agreement.

She had an idea percolating, however. "What if we cause a flood and wash them away?"

"How are you going to do that?" Pootie asked.

"Like this," Alexis retrieved the block of plastic explosive Pootie had given her as a meeting gift and used her nail to open the wrapping. "How much should I use to blow the outlet to the secondary tank?"

"How are you going to get it down there?" Boden asked before Pootie could reply.

Alexis held up a hand. "We'll get to that in a moment. Pootie?"

"I'm going to say keep it minimal after the mess we made of the gate," Pootie told her. "Especially if you're going to zap it instead of using a proper detonation method."

She watched as Alexis peeled off a thin curl and wrapped it in inert Etheric energy. "Maybe a bit more than that. You want to make sure the valve is destroyed but avoid blowing a hole in the tank."

Slash returned to their side of the main tank. "I don't know if you realize how bad the smell is."

"That's why we're targeting the secondary tank," Alexis assured her. "We want to cause a distraction. We don't want to make the specialists wade through unprocessed waste."

"I'm pretty sure they'd make us pay for it if we did," Sibil murmured unhappily.

The group watched intently as Alexis guided the translucent energy ball over to the valve that controlled the flow of water from the main tank to the secondary tank.

Alexis made the ball adhere to the valve and waited for everyone to get into position. "Ready?"

Gabriel kept his eyes on the walkway. "I'll say when."

Boden picked Pootie up and settled her onto his back in the space between his wings. The others lined up, ready to make the jump.

Alexis twisted the composition of the energy ball, triggering a sharp explosion that ripped the valve away.

Semi-processed water rushed from the open outlet and washed over the edge of the secondary tank, knocking the specialists off their feet.

"Move!" Gabriel commanded.

Boden took flight at the same instant the others leapt the gap between the pipe and the edge of the tank.

They heard angry yelling from below but didn't pause to find out whether they'd been seen. Alexis led the team along the wide curve of the rim at a sprint, aiming for the walkway Slash had found.

They tore down the walkway and into the maze, with the recovered specialists hurrying to catch them.

"Climb up!" K'aia called between heaving breaths. "We need to get to the surface!"

The team scaled the nearest tanks and continued running hell for leather along the top of them, utilizing the walkways that joined them.

Alexis remained in the lead, searching out the path of least resistance as they pounded along the walkways leading up and out of the central treatment plant.

Trey almost overbalanced when a suppression round hit his shoulder. He regained his equilibrium after a few sketchy steps and continued running.

The walkway gave way to a circular platform with a caged elevator. Boden swooped overhead without landing. "We haven't got much time!" he called to the others. "The specialists are gaining on us!"

Gabriel glanced around the platform and spotted an emergency ladder. "This way," he told them. "If we use the elevator, they'll just shut it down."

"Pootie, you're with me," K'aia told the Leian.

Pootie hopped down as Boden alighted and she jumped onto K'aia's back. "I owe you for this."

"Talk later," Gabriel told them as he mounted the ladder. "We have to keep moving."

Alexis took the rear, giving the others space before she collapsed the tunnel below her to block the specialists' pursuit.

The race continued as the team scaled the ladder double-time, ignoring the exits leading to the subterranean levels as they headed straight for the top of the tunnel.

The whine of the elevator followed them as they ascended, reminding them that the specialists were still chasing them.

"That's giving me the creeps," K'aia complained as she

concentrated on the awkwardness of maneuvering all four legs on the ladder. She craned her neck to see Alexis, which caused Pootie to curse.

"There's nothing we can do about it," Alexis panted. "Just keep moving!"

They reached the top of the ladder and emerged into an office building, scaring the workers into fleeing at the sight of ten mostly-armored combatants bursting into their workspace.

"Don't mind us!" Trey called cheerfully as he hurdled the desks in his way.

Gabriel noted that the elevator was already on their level and pulled up his map. "We're headed into an ambush," he told the team as they left the office and dashed along the corridor to the building exit. "Slow down."

"We don't have *time* to slow down!" Alexis argued. "We have less than twenty minutes on the clock until we fail." She skidded to a halt at the exit and peered out the barred window.

"Do you see them?" Sibil asked nervously.

Alexis nodded as she scanned the open street. "Yeah. Not just the ones who were after us, either."

K'aia joined Alexis at the window. "It looks like every specialist they have is out there. How did they get here so fast?"

Gabriel felt unaccustomed anger rising as he realized they were mere hundreds of feet from the endpoint. "They cheated."

The newer members of the team shrank back as the corridor was washed by the red light from Gabriel's eyes.

"They didn't cheat," Alexis told him softly. "But they're not playing fair, and what does Mom always say?"

"Mostly she says 'fucksticks' in this kind of situation," Trey chipped in. "Then she blasts them to dust and gets on with her day."

"I don't think that's an option," Alexis told him with regret.

Gabriel snorted and his eyes returned to normal. "Maybe not, but I'd feel good about it for a minute or two."

Alexis screwed her face up since she calculated the chances of them being able to fight their way through without losing anyone as being ridiculously low. "Gather in. I have an idea."

She grabbed Gabriel's hand to give herself a power boost and drew hard on the Etheric. The corridor lit up again as she concentrated on wrapping a shield around them all.

Jentek, Pootie, Boden, and Slash gaped as the energy encapsulated the team.

"Good call," Sibil enthused. "I wondered if you had any defensive skills with all that pew-pew you can do."

"Won't it break when they start shooting?" Jentek asked.

Alexis ground her teeth with the effort of stabilizing the shield. "Just don't step outside the bubble, and we should be fine."

She sent a flare out from the shield that knocked the door off its hinges. "Let's go."

The specialists opened fire the moment they stepped into the light.

The shield rippled, but it held. Alexis poured more energy into it as they walked toward the specialists. "Help me," she called. "I can't focus on walking while I'm holding this."

Gabriel wrapped his arm around his sister and stumbled when the contact increased her draw on him.

Trey laughed as he moved to help K'aia support Alexis and Gabriel. "We've got you. I sure as hell hope they're recording this."

The specialists were bumped out of their path by the shield as the team approached the endpoint.

Alexis disentangled herself to grasp the flag, ending the exercise. She waved it above her head, then sank to her knees with exhaustion as the specialists ceased fire.

Specialist Childers walked toward them with a smile. "Congratulations. You just earned yourselves a day's liberty." He waited for the cheers to die down. "Don't get too excited. You also just set the record for most candidates to complete the exercise. I want you in my office first thing the day after."

CHAPTER SEVEN

Zenith Station, Specialist Headquarters, War Room (two days later)

The holoscreen was paused on the image of the ten candidates walking through the perplexed specialists as though they were taking a pleasant stroll through Devon's bazaar on a Sunday morning.

The panel of high-ranking specialists had watched the video of the whole exercise from the team's point of view, and most just looked at them with astonishment.

Alexis and Gabriel listened as Torrence whispered his recommendation to the panel.

He wants us to skip ahead? Alexis wasn't sure how she felt about being separated from the unit.

They can't split us up, Gabriel replied. *It would cut our efficiency as a team.*

Specialist Childers laced his fingers on the table and fixed the twins with a conflicted look. "The two of you are putting me in a difficult situation. On the one hand, you're outstripping every learning resource we have. On the other, your unit still has ten months of training to get through before I can promote you."

Torrence snorted softly. "I told you they were going to be trouble," he murmured.

Childers gave him a sharp glance. "We don't need your opinion, Staff. This is a serious matter."

Torrence nodded respectfully and sat back in his chair. "You're right, but you know my recommendation. It's time they knew the whole truth about this war."

Specialist Childers pursed his lips. "That may be. However, this unit has no experience with live combat, so I cannot in good conscience send them into battle against the Kurtherian menace."

"Then prepare us," Gabriel requested in a low voice that nevertheless carried around the room. "Our reason for being is to take the fight to the Seven. They owe us blood."

Alexis got to her feet. "What he said. If you'd told us that the enemy was the Seven in the first place, we would have been even more motivated to get through the course."

K'aia and Trey added their agreement and sat down again. The others made similar statements, pledging their willingness to do whatever was in their power to take their vengeance on the destroyers of their homeworlds.

Specialist Childers waved down their enthusiastic promises to wipe the Kurtherians from the face of the universe. "I see we have something special with you ten. I hesitate to send you to your deaths. Return to your quarters and prepare for today's training. We will confer on your futures and call you back in when we have come to a decision."

. . .

Zenith Station, Candidate Quarters

Linda was waiting to pounce when the team arrived at their shared quarters. "What did you say to Indar and Draimond?" she demanded as Alexis came in behind the others.

The males in question were nowhere to be seen at that moment.

Alexis brushed Linda aside and walked over to her bunk. "If I were you, I'd be more concerned about how you treat them."

Linda followed her, seething visibly at the dismissal. "*Humans!*" she cursed. "You think you're so much better than every other species."

"Do you see us subjugating each other for kicks?" Gabriel asked.

Alexis noted a flash of guilt on the Torcellan's face before the supercilious mask dropped again.

Gabriel saw it as well. He caught Alexis' eye and tapped his temple with a finger before taking a seat at the card table in the rec area that split the room in two.

"I know humans talk endlessly about honor and have very little of it," Linda ground out between clenched teeth. "What right do you have to strip me of what little protection I have in this place?"

She flounced off to her unit's side of the room without waiting for a reply.

Alexis got Gabriel's meaning. She tuned into the Torcellan's inner thoughts, and her annoyance faded as she stumbled on the reason for Linda's acerbic nature; she was half-human and had been raised by only her mother. "Oh, crap," she murmured. "Couldn't you just be a standard asshole?"

She shared her findings with Gabriel, who winced as he realized what her early life would have been like for a Torcellan with an absent human father. *I don't know. Maybe we should try harder to work her out. Eve wouldn't have given her the backstory without a reason.*

I just wasn't expecting a side quest that involved talking an NPC through her traumatic childhood, Alexis countered. *What does that have to do with preparing for battle?*

K'aia left her conversation with Sibil and patted Alexis on the back. *Life lessons. They aren't always where you expect to find them.*

Alexis frowned and set off in Linda's direction. She ignored the sour look Linda gave her and took a seat on the locker at the end of her bed. "This is stupid. We should talk."

Linda scoffed. "About what?"

Alexis rested her chin on her hand and sighed. "We've got to get past this enmity. It's going to get us killed when we go to war."

Linda peered at Alexis, trying to work out if she was pulling something shady. "Why make the effort now? You've been pretty clear about not liking me."

Alexis bit back her retort. "It's not about personality clashes. It's about having the backs of everyone we're going to rely on, whether we like them or not."

Linda hesitated. "I don't work with humans."

"Because of your father." Alexis waited for Linda to reply. Seeing she wasn't going to open up, she decided to reach out. "I can't pretend I understand your life, even if I can read your mind and empathize. It's not fair that you were judged for your heritage, but you have to see that you're trapped in the cycle of judgment you've been subjected to."

Linda turned her back on Alexis, folding her arms protectively over her chest. When she spoke, her voice was laced with pent-up emotions. "Judged is right. Maybe…" Her voice trailed off, clearly unhappy with Alexis' intrusion despite the olive branch she was being offered. "You had no right to read my mind."

Alexis felt her face redden. "Yeah, well, you didn't give me much choice. I wouldn't want to see you dead just because you've been an ass."

Linda sighed, dropping her arms as she faced Alexis. "Okay. Say I work with you. What guarantee do I have that you won't stab me in the back when it matters? We're not through the cutting process yet."

Alexis shrugged. "You'll just have to trust that my word is good. I'm not here to compete with you or anyone else here. All I want is to—" She paused, seeing an opportunity to build that trust. "How about this? The enemy we're being trained to face is the Kurtherians. The Seven clans who want to remake this universe in their own image."

Linda's already-pale skin faded to ash. "The Kurtherians? How can we fight them? They're the most powerful species that has ever lived."

Alexis shook her head. "No, they're not. They might have power, but they fight amongst themselves for supremacy." She pushed thoughts of Gödel away. The Seven had not unified under her in the gameworld, as far as she was aware. "I'm the daughter of the Empress. I know exactly how they're weak. We can beat them if we're united."

Linda was silent for a long moment as she processed everything Alexis had told her.

Gabriel spoke up in Alexis' mind. *Don't push. She's going to come around. I can feel it.*

Alexis glanced at her brother and nodded minutely. She forced herself to stay calm and wait, despite her burning desire to hear what Linda had to say.

Linda suddenly sprang into action, extending a hand to Alexis with a serious smile. "Allies. I can do that."

Alexis accepted the handshake with a hard smile of her own. "I'm glad. Allies."

She returned to their rec area, feeling like she'd made progress in a way that didn't exactly make sense. But if Linda stayed true to her word like Alexis intended to, she would be satisfied.

Trey leaned over to Gabriel, keeping his cards covered. "I didn't expect that to go down that way. I thought once females had a grudge, they built a wall around it and nurtured it forever."

Alexis slapped him upside the head fondly as she passed. "Don't be so sexist. I don't see you and Ch'Irzt kissing and making up."

Trey rubbed the back of his head with a look of distaste on his face. "Yeah, but in the asshole stakes, Linda is a few hundred levels below my cousin."

"True," K'aia agreed. "But maybe you could take steps to remedy that."

Trey grinned. "I suppose I could beat some decency into him when I get out of here."

Gabriel laughed. "That would be a beginning. Social skills have to start somewhere."

Alexis sighed and rolled her eyes. "Or, you could try talking him down from his jealousy. He's a decent fighter, and we're going to need a crew for the *Gemini* once we get back to the real world. You only get one family."

Trey snorted. "You guys are my family."

Alexis fixed him with a sharp look. "Four people do not make a crew. Don't you want our parents to feel comfortable about us joining the fight for real? 'We have a crew and the means to fight independently' is a much more attractive proposition than, 'Hey, can the four of us go tear shit up on our own?'"

Trey made a face. "Yeah, but *Ch'Irzt*? I think I'd rather stay home."

A message from Eve put an end to the conversation.

Gabriel dropped his cards and jumped to his feet. "Finally! I thought they were never going to call us."

He left the table and headed for the door. "Come on, Alexis. You know the time difference."

Alexis followed him, leaving Trey and K'aia to finish their game.

"You're not going?" K'aia asked Trey.

He shook his head. "No. I spoke to Mahi' already this week. She won't be there. What about you?"

"Not my parents," K'aia told him. "Let the twins have their time."

Sibil wandered over and took Gabriel's empty seat. "Deal me in. I have a question. What happens when our unit gets promoted?"

Gorrak heard her and came over. "You think that's what the bosses are going to decide?"

Sibil lifted a shoulder. "I can't see why not. They'll

probably have us skip ahead, at least. We've proven we're tight as a unit. I mean, we beat the specialists without any problem thanks to our combined efforts. Why would they keep us here when there's a war happening out there?"

There was a murmur of agreement from the rest of the unit. They gathered around the table, Pootie pushing her way to the front of the group.

"We are not ready." Boden's gentle voice was soothing despite the finality of his tone. "Almost, but we still have a ways to go before we can fight Kurtherians."

K'aia glanced at Trey. "My concern is which modified species' they're using to fight for them."

"At least it's not going to be the Ookens," Trey countered.

"How do we know that?" K'aia argued. "If we don't get in some practice against the tentacle-fest, we're not going to be at our most effective when we face them for real."

"What the hell is an Ooken?" Pootie asked.

Trey spread his arms wide and waved them in a poor approximation. "Imagine I was a few feet taller and had a bunch of tentacles," he began to the horror of the group. "I'm not done. They have razor-sharp teeth in place of suckers, and they're slaved to the Kurtherians' will."

Trey and K'aia looked up as the group froze and a shimmer passed over the room.

"What was that?" Trey asked.

K'aia shrugged, unperturbed. "Beats the crap out of me. Ask Eve."

They received a single line of text in their internal HUDs.

Ask and you shall receive. Game updated to include the Ookens as an antagonist. — xo Eve

Trey cursed heartily as the game was reactivated. "Okay, so we need to be ready for the Ookens. Good."

Sibil laughed. "What, battling Kurtherians wasn't enough for you?"

"Not even," Trey told her with as much sincerity as he'd ever felt in his life. "The harder we're pushed, the better chance we have of surviving."

Another message arrived, this one from Specialist Childers.

"We've been summoned," Pootie remarked with some surprise. "That was fast."

CHAPTER EIGHT

The twins rejoined the unit in the corridor outside Specialist Headquarters.

"I'm shaking," Sibil admitted. "I don't know whether I want to hear we're being promoted early or that we've got to stay on track and complete the course."

Alexis lifted a shoulder. "Either way, things are about to get stepped up a level. We've proven our value as a unit twice over."

The door opened, and SI Torrence popped his head out. "Specialist Childers will see you now."

SI Torrence stood at ease by the door while the candidates filed into the war room, each with a varying degree of nervousness and a vague expectation of some unknowable adventure to be revealed.

Specialist Childers smiled warmly as they entered. "Take a seat, candidates."

Alexis caught a stray thought that revealed his gruffness to be the mask he wore to protect himself from the burden of leading the program and knowing that the majority of the fresh-faced candidates would die before the end of their first deployment.

She smiled back as she took a seat in the first row of chairs facing the curved table where the lead specialist sat alone.

Specialist Childers resumed his seriousness once the unit was seated. "The decision of what to do with your unit was not an easy one. We feel it would be wasteful to have you continue on the same track as the rest of your intake group. You are clearly a cohesive and effective unit beyond what is expected at this stage of the course, and that your combined strengths and knowledge make a whole much greater than the sum of its parts is clear to us all. However, we also recognize that it would be a pitfall if one of you is lost on the battlefield."

He paused to let his words sink in.

Alexis read the subtext with disappointment. *We're not being sent to the battlefield,* she told Gabriel, K'aia, and Trey. *My guess is we're going to get the promotion and be sent for more specialized training.*

"Our decision is that you will be promoted," Specialist Childers announced. "But that you will spend six months with the recruitment teams instead of the usual two. It is our reasoning that this will give you the opportunity to strengthen your knowledge of each other's specialties, with the exception of course of the Nacht candidates' natural connection to the Etheric realm."

Dimension, Alexis corrected mentally.

Shh! K'aia hissed. *This is important.*

"You will return to your current assigned quarters," the specialist continued. "Testing will continue between deployments. We want to ensure the rigors of your assignments are not detracting from your growth as operatives. Do you have any questions, specialists?"

Gabriel indicated he wanted permission to speak.

"Go ahead," Specialist Childers acknowledged.

"Whose oversight will our unit be under if we're being taken out of the standard track?" Gabriel inquired.

Specialist Childers nodded toward SI Torrence. "Staff Instructor Torrence has agreed to act in a supervisory role while you are in this…hardening phase."

Alexis frowned at the phrase. It sounded to her like their experience was going to be every bit as exacting as being sent to the front lines. She raised her hand and received a nod from Specialist Childers. "When will we be deployed?"

"Immediately," Specialist Childers replied. "There are always planets in need of our intervention, and one we believe will suffice for your first assignment has just come to our attention. You will leave this room and report to Supply. Once you are equipped, you will report to SI Torrence at the Deck Zero transfer bay."

He swept the newly-minted specialists with a sharp gaze, and seeing there were no further questions, dismissed the unit. "Specialists," he called as they filed out of the war room. "I wish you all the luck of your deities. May you avoid meeting them for a long time to come."

Alexis heard the tiredness in the specialist's tone and turned back to offer him a firm smile. As she left, she sent him her certainty that they would not only survive but thrive under whatever conditions they met.

· · ·

Open Space, Zenith Battleship *ZI II*

SI Torrence switched off the holoscreen, ending his recap of the mission objectives as they got within sight of their target planet. "Okay, guys. Does anyone have any questions about what we're going to do?"

The unit was collectively silent, lending the transport bay they'd been assigned upon boarding an oppressive air. Their orders were clear enough. Land, suppress any negative reactions to their presence, and save as many fit and healthy citizens of fighting age as they were able to while causing minimal physical harm in the process.

"It's not looking good for them that they have no planetary security," Gabriel commented as he checked his issued gear.

Alexis had to agree. "Especially since we had to divert to avoid the fighting in the next system over." She attached multiple gas canisters to her rig, pushing aside her discomfort at the negative association she had with them as she did so. "What do you think we're going to find when we get down there?"

"Frightened people," K'aia told them without inflection. "We're going to be invaders to them, just like the specialists who conscripted us were until we learned better."

Trey remained quiet. His mind was caught up in battling his urge to reject their orders and do something to work with the people on the planet instead of forcing them into a life in the military.

Alexis couldn't help pick up the fractious thoughts Trey was broadcasting. She put her hand on his shoulder. "I know," she told him gently. "I don't like it either. None of us do. But this is the only way, I think."

"Is it?" Trey countered. "Or can we find a better way that doesn't infringe on the rights of these people to choose their own path?"

Alexis shrugged. "I can't see one," she admitted. "The Seven are too close. We're too late to make any attempt at diplomacy."

Gabriel saw similar discomfort in the postures of everyone in the bay. "I don't think any of us like it. It's too close to what we went through." He paused as a thought occurred. "Hey, do you think the team who nabbed us felt like this?"

SI Torrence nodded, hearing their murmurings as he walked past them to the drop ramp controls. "Nobody I know feels entirely okay with plucking people from their lives, but we can't spare the fighters to place protection around every planet in the Seven's way. All we can do is our best to save who we can and fight them off when they attack."

The landing went without incident. No law enforcement or military came screaming out to meet the unit when they debarked far outside the planet's center of population, largely thanks to the stealth technology that hid their ships.

SI Torrence held them back and gave last-minute instructions while the other units assigned to the mission landed and got into position. "Keep to the route set on your dash-comm. Your drop point is half a day's drive from the city, with four stops along the way. Don't get separated from each other, and don't take any risks if the people fight back. Use your gas if a crowd turns into a mob." He paused, his face softening as he looked at each of them in turn. "Remember, I'm here to guide you. You get stuck, you call me."

The unit approached their vehicles, two smallish ships with separated rear compartments. The front had room for five, with a shaped bench at the back for the larger or four-legged species. The cockpit was laid out somewhere between a fighter Pod's and a truck's, with the pilot's and navigator's chairs in front of the hybrid dash-comm and benches behind, with all the dangling straps they expected to see in military transports.

Alexis stepped aside to allow Gabriel the pilot's chair, wanting time to think while they made their way to the ground. K'aia climbed in behind her, followed by Trey and Boden.

There was a moment of discontent when Slash and Sibil clashed over who would pilot the second ship.

"You're not flying this thing," Sibil argued. "We'll be dead before you manage to take off."

"Says you!" Slash retorted.

They were both cut short when Gorrak slipped around them and hopped into the coveted seat. "Quit stressing. It doesn't matter who flies it, except it's going to be me."

Both females shot the Shrillexian looks that would kill a lesser being.

He just shrugged and jerked a thumb toward the passenger bench behind him. "You can keep Jentek company," he told Slash. "Sibil, you can navigate."

The Leath looked up from his quiet conversation with Pootie at the sound of his name. "Huh?"

Pootie rolled her eyes as she moved over to make room for the surly Noel-ni. "You suck, Gorrak."

"Yeah, and Slash'd crash us," he replied. "Face it, I'm the best driver out of the five of us."

Nobody had an argument for that since Gorrak had proven to be the best of them all during driver training.

They set off in convoy toward their first designated target in speculative silence.

Gabriel concentrated on the dash-comm and the road. He felt confident, and his mind was clear of doubt as he drove the route that took them through the rolling agricultural land.

He'd had time to think about his realization that a person of duty and honor had little room to maneuver since he'd gone through the archives as SI Torrence had instructed. His love of history had always been confined to who won what battle, and how hard they'd kicked the ass of the enemy.

His trip through the archives had left him introspective while he worked to figure out why it took so little time for people of all species to forget the lessons they'd learned the hard way and jump right back into repeating the same mistakes. Before the planets whose governments had been smart enough to pull together had formed a defense, this whole galaxy had been at risk of being lost to the clan who'd earmarked it as a rich source of life to play their sick games with.

His conclusion was simple: conscription might not be the ideal way to ensure the Seven didn't overrun this part of the universe, but it sure beat the people of the game-world rolling over and showing them their bellies.

He saw the immorality in forcing choices on the people, but something his mother had once told him and

Alexis had helped him reconcile his feelings on the situation.

Survival came first, and whatever price they had to pay for freedom was only a fraction of its worth.

They would leave this game with an intimate understanding of what it cost to enforce the hard decisions a leader had to make for the good of everyone. The incentive was that humanity and their allies were the innocents at risk in the real-world analog of this scenario.

Alexis, however, found herself leaning toward the other end of the argument. She didn't know if she was capable of causing harm, even if it was for the greater good. She glanced at Gabriel's cool exterior and felt the calm radiating from him. *How are you not a mess?* she asked him in their mindspace.

Gabriel lifted a shoulder without taking his eyes off the road. *Easy,* he replied. *Soon as Trey told us that Eve altered the program to include Ookens, I knew the Seven were bound to take the people of this planet and twist them into abominations. You're the math genius. We can't save everyone, and there aren't enough resources to evacuate a whole planet. We have to follow the plan.*

Alexis pressed her lips together. She was torn between the need to preserve even a small piece of the civilization on this planet and her strong belief that individual rights were as important as the good of the many.

There was no way to offer them the choice with the Zenith model of operations.

She gazed out the window, seeing none of the alien construction they passed as their ships ate up the miles. She barely noted the people she saw working the fields, except to acknowledge that they were prime targets for the Seven, being tall and well-built for hard labor.

Trey leaned between the twins' seats. "How far are we from the first town?" he asked, craning to see the dash-comm. His face dropped when he saw they were nearing the first marker, then hardened when he saw the people of the planet for the first time and it hit him that all of them were going to be wiped out by the Seven. "They look so peaceful. I hate that we have to do this to them."

K'aia spoke for the first time since they'd set off. "Take it from me. The people we save will be grateful eventually."

Trey turned to give her a confused look. "How can you say that?"

K'aia inclined her head. "I can say it because I've been on both sides of the situation. Did I ever tell you about what I did in the time between leaving the mine and deciding to find my way to Bethany Anne?"

Trey shook his head, curious at his usually stoic friend's sudden verbosity. "Some? Not really."

K'aia drew a long breath and exhaled the ghost of her grief. "I went back to my home and buried my dead. I searched City-on-the-Lake for any surviving members of my family and found none. For a while, I was alive, but I didn't live. I felt guilty that I had lived and my family didn't." She shifted on the bench. "I spent some time doing my best to remedy that before Sabine set me on the right track, but eventually I got to where I could see that I'd been given a chance to do something bigger with my life. Something that mattered."

"I get that," Sibil told her in a low voice. "It started with feeling good about being able to fight, but when we learned in class how the Seven operate, I went to check the archives. I found out that they'd worked their genocide program on my homeworld, and it made me forget I was pissed at the turn my life had taken. Now my only focus is on making sure others get the same chance to take the fight to them that we have been given."

Slash bumped Sibil with her shoulder. "I can't say the same. My people are safe back in the Empire. Whether they disowned me or not, I'm glad the Empress has their backs. But I'm glad I got conscripted. I was only heading for prison or an early grave. Now I have a legitimate focus for my aggression."

"I hear *that*," Gorrak called over the comm.

"Are we there yet?" Pootie asked.

CHAPTER NINE

Alexis closed the rear doors on the sleeping people and headed back into the cockpit of the ship, feeling like her soul had been soiled in some indescribable way.

Non-player characters or not, nothing about the activity she'd just partaken in made her feel like a good person. Not the terrified expressions on the faces of the ones too shocked to fight back, and definitely not that they'd been left with no choice but to use force on those who had been cognizant of the danger the team presented on their arrival in the town.

"We could have handled that better," Gabriel agreed, feeling the same grubbiness deep inside he felt coming from his twin.

The town square was empty as they drove away, the remaining people having fled when they realized they had no chance against the fully-armored strangers who had appeared in a cloud of purple gas and taken their pick of the young and strong.

K'aia did what she could to comfort the others, despite

her own feelings of ineptitude in the face of their inexperienced fumbling of the objective. "We don't have to feel good about it. We just saved a bunch of lives. Doesn't matter one bit that we did it by force."

"Oh, it matters," Trey countered. "It matters because we're not heartless. I hope it never gets easier to bear than this because that will mean we've lost what makes us the good guys."

That more than anything gave them solace as they worked their way through stopping points two and three. Two hours into the drive toward their final stop, the dash-comm beeped and SI Torrence's concerned face replaced the route map.

"Stop where you are," he instructed. "There's been a development."

Gabriel pulled over to the side of the road, and Gorrak halted the other ship beside them and opened the side window so they could all listen together.

SI Torrence's voice had a strange quality to it, coming from both ships' speaker systems at once. "Stay exactly where you are," he told them. "The fighting has spilled over into this system. We're pulling you out."

Gabriel narrowed his eyes at the unexpected news. "What do you mean, you're pulling us out? Why?"

"The Seven have sent their soldiers down to the planet," SI Torrence replied. "They know we're here, and standard procedure is to abandon the mission and extract all specialists still on world."

Alexis balked at the thought of leaving the people they hadn't yet rescued to die at the hands—or tentacles—of whoever the Seven was using to hunt them. "Staff, we can fight them," she told him. "This is what we've been training for."

Gabriel nodded at the flickering holoscreen. "Yeah. It'll sure as hell beat what we've been doing all day. Let us stay."

"Please," Trey finished for them all.

SI Torrence shook his head, his face set in firm lines. "Absolutely not. Even if you are capable of beating them, we've invested too much in your training. You're too valuable to risk."

"Screw that!" K'aia's outburst was accompanied by exclamations of outrage from the rest of the unit.

Pootie scrambled over the benches and through the gap between Alexis and Gabriel's seats and pointed a finger at SI Torrence. "Don't make us start a mutiny down here."

Alexis calmed Pootie with a hand. "What Pootie is *trying* to say is, can't you contact Specialist Childers and ask permission for us to use this as further training?"

Gabriel grinned as he figured out Alexis' tactic. "Yeah, training. How many are they sending? If it's a small number, it will give us the opportunity to put into practice everything you and the specialists have taught us without the risk of being part of the main battle."

SI Torrence looked at the twins like he wasn't entirely sure whether he was being played.

"No, really," Alexis insisted. "Think about it. We get to demonstrate Etheric Empire fighting techniques, mixed in with the tactical and strategic knowledge we've learned on the Zenith course."

SI Torrence faltered, caught between his duty to follow procedure and his desire to see the best students he'd ever had in action.

"We'll bring back any Kurtherian technology we get our hands on," Alexis added in a quiet voice, dipping her head. She hoped the trick of human psychology worked on Yollins, too—or at least on Yollin NPCs programmed by Eve.

SI Torrence frowned and muted the call. They waited impatiently while he lifted a handset to his ear and spoke inaudibly.

"What's he saying, Alexis?" Trey murmured.

Alexis found it hard to read the SI's rapidly-moving lips, but she persisted. "He's talking to Specialist Childers. I think...I think he's arguing our case?" She squinted in frustration since the handset partially blocked her view. "Dammit. I can't tell what he's saying!"

Their agony was ended a moment later when SI Torrence restored the audio and gave them a solemn nod. "You'd better not make me look like a liar."

Gabriel grinned. "Sweet! Does that mean we get to fight?"

"Orders are to make your way to the hills and find a place to lay low," SI Torrence told them, his hologram bouncing as he ran. "I'll be there in half an hour, forty minutes maximum. Specialist Childers wants to be sure you're equipped for this, and somebody needs to get the people you're transporting to safety."

He signed off, and Gabriel and Gorrak got the ships moving again.

"Follow me," Gorrak called over the comm.

"Yeah, *hell*, no!" Gabriel exclaimed, speeding up to overtake Gorrak as they turned off the highway onto a beaten track. "Eat my dust!"

Alexis was amused by the unusual spike of annoyance from her brother. *What's got your panties in a twist?* she inquired with a chuckle.

Sooner we get there, the longer we have to strategize, he replied.

Alexis giggled at Gabriel's attitude, sensing the real reason he was suddenly showing his caveman side. *Didn't realize Gorrak's driving skill had become a sore point with you.*

Shhh! Gabriel told her. *I'm trying to concentrate here.*

Alexis shrugged and sat back to enjoy the race. Their ships were fitted with inertia-countering technology for situations where they'd have to go off-road at speed, so their passengers would be just fine. *Oookay, Dad.*

Gabriel ignored her and swerved left to go around a rock that split the dirt road in two.

Gorrak went right, and the two ships met on the other side with a shower of sparks as they scraped past each other. Gabriel nudged ahead to take the lead as the path narrowed.

Alexis gave her brother a pointed look. "Why not just crash now so we can walk all the way?" she snarked.

Gabriel sighed and opened the comm. "Take it down a notch before we damage the ships," he told Gorrak as he reduced his speed to something more sensible.

Farmland gave way to wilder vegetation, and the ground grew uneven and rocky. They took their ships as high as they dared, straddling the line between keeping up their speed and remaining undetected by the enemy ship they saw in the distance on the dash-comm.

Alexis wondered if the enemy ship was headed for the

city, or maybe it had honed in on the location of another unit.

Either way, they were safe for now. Their ships dropped out of sight as the hills rose out of seemingly nowhere. Gabriel called a halt once they were enclosed by craggy stone walls whose sharp edges had been softened by erosion.

Trey checked their time and left his seat with the idea of putting a meal together. "Is everyone hungry?" he asked.

"Want a hand?" K'aia offered over the enthusiastic assent that came over the comm from the other ship.

Trey waved her off. "I'm good, thanks. It's just rehydrating whatever they packed in for us. I'll call everyone when I'm done."

"We'll eat outside," Alexis decided. "There's barely room to swing a Noel-ni in here."

Trey wasn't against the idea after being cooped up in the cockpit for most of the day. "Sounds good to me." He left the cockpit and headed for the galley.

K'aia got to her feet as a thought occurred. "One of us should check on the passengers. I'll be back soon."

Trey took a moment when he got to the galley to look through the options before settling on making a version of the human dish called chili. His thoughts were on the battle ahead as he emptied various sachets of dehydrated ingredients into a deep, two-handled pot and added water before turning on the heat and placing the lid on the pot to seal it.

There was some analogy to be made between cooking and planning a fight, he thought. Success depended on prior preparation, for example. It had been months by their time since Addix had died, but he saw how her loss still affected the twins. Even K'aia still grew introspective when the Ixtali's name came up, but she had been the spymistress' protégé so it was to be expected. He hadn't known Addix well. In fact, he'd been mostly terrified of her as an instructor who gave no quarter, but his determination to repay her for saving his mother's life was no less strong for the lack of bonding between them.

This was a huge step in the right direction. Manipulating the game into pushing them ahead had been too easy for Alexis. He was certain it was the right choice, however. The longer they were in here, the closer everyone in the real world got to that confrontation. He for one didn't want to miss his chance to pay the Seven back for the destruction of Qu'Baka.

There was enough to feed a whole battalion by the time he'd finished cooking the chili and baked a batch of bread from pre-made dough.

K'aia appeared at the galley door, drawn by the aroma. "The passengers are all good. I gave them an extra dose of the gas to make sure they don't wake up before SI Torrence gets them to the transfer, however they're doing it from here. You about done with dinner?"

Trey nodded. "Yeah. Grab that for me," he requested, indicating the box he'd loaded up with their mess tins, spoons, ten bottles of rehydrated milk, and the bread.

"Gotcha." K'aia picked up the box and followed Trey as he carried the pot outside and set it down on the center of the flat rock the others had appropriated as a makeshift table.

"Grub's up," Trey called. "Get it while it's both kinds of hot."

"What's that supposed to mean?" Sibil asked. "How can it be more than one kind of hot?"

"You haven't had chili before? There's heat-hot and spicy-hot." Alexis chuckled as she plucked a tin and a spoon from the box and headed over to sniff the contents of the pot. "It's pretty mild right now, but trust me, this stuff gets spicier the longer you leave it."

There was a scramble for the food, then a few minutes of silence while they filled their stomachs.

"'S good," Sibil mumbled through her first mouthful.

"It's one of my favorites from human cuisine," Trey told her. He passed out the bread and took a seat on the mossy ground to eat his dinner. "So, we persuaded the big man to let us fight. What next?"

Gabriel swallowed and took a sip of the questionable-tasting milk. Still, it calmed the capsaicin party happening in his mouth, so he sucked it up and sipped again. "My thinking is that we track down that ship we saw and take it over."

Alexis tilted her head, a wicked gleam appearing in her eyes. "I have another idea. How about we call Gemini?"

The rest of the unit looked at her blankly, while Gabriel, K'aia, and Trey broke into similar grins.

"That's if she can get here in time," Gabriel hedged. "Do we know how many Gates we are from Devon?"

Alexis shrugged. "I already called her, so…"

"She'll get here, or she won't," Gabriel finished for her.

"You've got it," she answered, refocusing her attention on her food. "Hey, Trey, this is pretty good."

"You say that like you were expecting it to be bad," Trey told her with narrowed eyes.

Alexis picked up her milk and shook the bottle vigorously. "I tasted my milk first. I'll be honest, I wasn't expecting much from the chili."

"Enough about the food," Pootie cut in. "Who is Gemini?"

"Our battleship," the twins answered in unison.

"You have a *what*, now?" Sibil asked. "Why are we only just hearing about this?"

"Yeah," Gorrak added. "What I want to know is why you didn't call it sooner."

Gabriel lifted a shoulder as he stirred his chili. "We didn't need her while we were on Zenith."

"But at the Corral?" Gorrak pressed. "We could have escaped at any time if we'd had a freaking *battleship* to swoop in and pick us up."

"Didn't want to escape," Gabriel reminded him. "We chose this path."

A movement overhead caused them to all look up. They spotted a Zenith ship and went back to eating, secure in the knowledge that it was only SI Torrence coming in to land.

The ship landed a little way from theirs, and SI Torrence came down the ramp with four antigrav carts trundling behind him like a high-tech version of baby ducks following their mama.

He glanced at their makeshift camp with approval. "Glad to see you thought to refuel before you go in," he praised.

Alexis snorted. "I was just thinking of taking a nap when you arrived, Staff."

The joke brought chuckles from the others. Alexis craned to see what was in the carts without getting up. "It looks like you brought us some goodies."

"Goodies, indeed," SI Torrence agreed. "Those of you with mech certification will find what you need in the cargo bay of my ship. The rest of you, I brought battle armor."

K'aia, Trey, Sibil, Gorrak, Pootie, Jentek, Boden, and Slash dashed to the Zenith ship.

"I'm good," Alexis decided. "I don't need to be confined to a cabin. It doesn't suit my fighting style."

Gabriel paused in his tracks and stepped off the ramp, sighing at the missed opportunity. "I stay with Alexis," he told the staff instructor. "She's right. We'll fight better without the mechs. We'll take point on the unit."

"I thought you'd say that," Torrence told them with a smile. "I brought a set of armor for each of you, plus weapons."

Alexis stood and stretched before walking over to get a good look at the contents of the cart Torrence indicated for her. Her eyes widened. "What kind of armor is this?" she asked in amazement, touching the bright blue metal to see if it felt as warm as it looked.

"Experimental," Torrence told her. "It's up to you whether you take it or go with the standard issue you're wearing now."

"What are the drawbacks?" Alexis asked.

Torrence shrugged. "We don't know yet. You two are the only ones with the ability to use this armor to its full capability. The idea is that you can move freely between here and the Etheric while wearing it."

Alexis met Gabriel's gaze with identical wide eyes. *You think this is Jean's prototype for the Bl'kheth armor?* she asked him.

Gabriel couldn't see that it was anything else. *It would make sense to have us test it in a simulation before putting it out there for real,* he replied. *The question is, will it work?*

Alexis grinned. "Only one way to find out," she told him aloud, drawing a confused look from SI Torrence. "Let's get it on and find out."

CHAPTER TEN

The twins emerged from their ground ships wearing the new armor.

Alexis flexed her armor, unused to the way the suit worked with every movement of her body.

"It's amazing, right?" Gabriel remarked, performing a similar set of stretches to test his armor's capabilities.

"I don't know yet," Alexis told him. "Let's see how bad the drag is in the Etheric before we start singing its praises."

She slipped into the Etheric, bracing herself for the usual increased draw on her energy.

Gabriel joined her a fraction of a second later.

They looked at each other and grinned.

Alexis called out. "Eve, can we get a minute?"

There was a swirl in the mists ahead of them, and Eve walked out. "What can I help you with?" she asked.

Alexis extended a hand and manifested an energy ball to see how it felt to draw through the armor instead of her own body. "Are we right about this being the first build with the Bl'kheth armor?"

Eve smiled beatifically. "The sixth, actually. Jean isn't going to waste resources on building the real armor until it's been thoroughly tested in simulation, meaning, she wants you to push it to its limits."

Gabriel chuckled. "I can't see that will be an issue. Do you have any hints as to what's ahead in the game? It would be better not to die of surprise." He grinned. "For the test, of course."

Eve fixed him with a stern look. "You might be able to wrap Izanami around your little finger with that smile, but you're getting nothing out of me, Gabriel John Nacht."

"Ooh, she used your Sunday name!" Alexis teased. "Thank you, Eve. We'll manage from here. Just one thing. How are you getting Ookens if there's no Gödel in this timeline to create them?"

"Evolution works in the funniest ways," Eve told her with a mysterious smile. She dropped her hands to her hips. "Go on now, or the battle will start without you."

SI Torrence breathed a sigh of relief when the twins reappeared in the clearing. "I thought… Never mind what I thought." He waved the unit in, no easy feat when eight of them wore the fifteen-foot tall mech suits. "This is the latest data on the invaders. They've sent two ships. Both have landed in the city I had you avoid earlier. It's looking like they've sent in their shock troops, mindless killing machines with only one goal—to consume any organic material they come across."

"Doesn't that include the plants and animals?" Trey

asked, picturing an Ooken chewing up a tree trunk while the people around ran to safety.

SI Torrence shook his head. "If that were the case, they'd be easily distracted. They go for movement, which is just about perfect since the first thing any sensible person would do on seeing one of these monsters is run for their lives."

"Then I guess we're a bunch of dumbasses," K'aia called with a laugh. "Because we're going to make mush out of them." She had her mech stamp the ground and grind its heel afterward. "All that's going to be left is paste."

That raised a cheer from the others, who had their mechs copy her movements.

Alexis raised an eyebrow. "If you're all done with the dance audition, we should get started before the city is lost." She grabbed a utility belt loaded with grenades from the antigrav cart holding the weapons and attached it around her waist before selecting a pair of short-barrel rifles to accompany them. "You ready?"

Gabriel completed his own rifling of the weapons stash and came up with a compound bow and a full quiver. He slung the quiver over his back, being careful not to dislodge any of his knives. "G-2-G, sis." He hopped onto Trey's mech and climbed up to its left shoulder. "But I'm not wasting my energy walking."

Trey lifted the enormous sword in his mech's right hand and roared his readiness. "Let's go!"

Alexis hopped onto the hand K'aia lowered and took her position on the mech's shoulder. "Move out."

The mechs ate up the miles without difficulty, bringing them in range of the city limits in just over an hour.

The city was already in flames, telling them that the Ookens had been wreaking havoc there for some time.

Alexis was disheartened that they hadn't gotten there in time to prevent the destruction that had already occurred, but she was also aware that they had plenty of time to save the majority of the population.

She stood up and accessed the Etheric, using the energy to make herself rise until she had a three-sixty view of the city streets. She opened her mind to locate the hive mind of the Ookens and was surprised to find no trace of it in the mindspace. "Of course," she muttered. "Why make it easy on us?"

"Where are we headed?" Gabriel called over the comm, interrupting her private bitching session.

Alexis shaded her eyes against the setting sun and scanned for sound. She located the most recent outbreak of violence by the sounds of despair coming from the people. "That way," she directed, pointing to the east side of the grid. "I can hear people screaming."

The mechs crashed through fallen buildings and rubble-choked streets to the source of the screams Alexis had pinpointed. The unit had trained for this moment.

They stomped the Ookens guarding the gates of the park where the people had gathered in the mistaken belief they'd be safe, then fanned out, laying down bursts of suppressive fire on the roving bands of enemies to help the people escape.

The people cried out in relief when they saw the giant mechanical monsters were there to help. It took them less than a moment to start running for the streets now that their way wasn't being blocked by murderous, tentacled soldiers.

"Keep the civilians covered," Alexis ordered as she began blasting the weird-looking Ookens with thick gouts of flames.

The unit kept their mechs moving, splattering Ookens under their heavy clawed feet as they followed Alexis' direction.

Alexis was glad her team had the protection of the mech suits. These Ookens seemed to have more intelligence than the kind they'd learned about in the real world. They also used weapons, each having a laser rifle in addition to the ever-biting teeth in their tentacles. She noted the soldiers recognized that the unit was a danger by the way they moved, darting in to mob the mechs, then firing wildly on them as they dashed back. "We need to get some strategy going on here," she told Gabriel.

"Agreed. We can herd them." Gabriel braced his feet and fired the explosive arrows in his quiver to blast a ditch into the ground around them.

Trey helped as best he could, although his efforts produced gaping holes in the landscape rather than the line Gabriel was drawing to keep their enemy contained. He shrugged, almost dislodging Gabriel as his mech mimicked the action. "Sorry!" he called. "How many do you think there are?"

"Too many for my liking," Gabriel replied. "I'm going down there."

Trey wasn't too sure that was a good idea until he saw that Gabriel was doing something with the Etheric to make his body incorporeal.

Gabriel phased in and out of sight, and Ookens dropped wherever he appeared.

Alexis lowered herself to the ground and joined Gabriel in his decimation of the enemy troops. She barely felt the impact of their tentacles on her armor, registering that the inertia blocking she had become used to in earlier models had been improved.

Gabriel grinned as she reached his position. "This is the life, right?" he enthused as he tore two tentacles off an Ooken and used them to beat back the others surrounding them. "You feel like getting fancy?"

"Always," Alexis replied with a giggle at the Ookens being knocked back by his efforts. She loosed a concussive wave that tore into the Ookens and gave them space to maneuver. "What do you have in mind?"

Gabriel furrowed his brow, considering their options. "Link to me. I have an idea."

Alexis harnessed her power to Gabriel's, seeing the seed of a daring plan bloom in the recesses of his mind. "Just don't blow us up, okay?"

Gabriel grunted as he took control of the energy Alexis handed him. "You might wanna put a shield around us because this is going to get messy."

Alexis siphoned a small amount of energy from the river she was pulling from the Etheric for Gabriel and cocooned them within it. "Done."

Gabriel continued to spool out the energy until he felt like his skin would split from the pressure, then released it in a burning wave that turned the Ookens for thirty feet in all directions to ashes.

"Nice!" came the cheer from K'aia.

Pootie, meanwhile, was tearing her own strip from the enemy's hides. She and Trey worked to stay together, with Trey keeping her mech protected while she fed explosive after explosive from her stash into the tubes meant for kinetics.

The ground shook with the impacts, knocking the Ookens off their feet. Trey mopped up around her with wide sweeps of his sword.

Over at the west gate, K'aia had plucked a tall tree and was using it as a staff. Her mech danced a deadly ballet, with Boden and Slash in the roles of backup dancers.

Boden's mech jumped to clear K'aia's staff. "Careful!" he cried.

"Oops!" K'aia called. "Didn't see you there."

"How could you miss me?" Boden groused. "I'm as large as you!"

"Kinda concentrating on the fight," K'aia replied distractedly. "See if you can help Sibil and Gorrak."

She pointed with the tree trunk at the southeast side of the park, where their teammates had gotten themselves into something of a jam.

Their mechs were pinned against a building, which Jentek had climbed. They were prevented from moving by their need to protect the group of civilians who had run into the building, thinking to find safety there.

The Leath reached the roof and began firing on the crowd of Ookens trapping Sibil and Gorrak. "Damn civilians," he cursed. "Why they couldn't run in a direction that didn't trap them, I don't know!"

"Never mind that!" Sibil exclaimed. "Just keep firing!"

Pootie and Boden arrived to back them up, and the Ooken group was quickly picked off.

"Whose idea was it to stay and fight?" Pootie bitched. "Because I'm going to save one of my charges to stick up their—"

She was cut off by an explosion nearby.

Everyone in the park looked up as a dark ship blocked the remaining light.

"Great!" Pootie yelled. "More of them!"

The ship slowed overhead and opened its drop doors to disgorge yet more troops.

"More Ookens?" Alexis asked.

"No!" Pootie exclaimed. "They don't have the tentacles."

Alexis let off a stream of curses more suited to her mother when she realized what they faced next. "Mechs!"

"Could be worse," Gabriel told her. "At least it's not zombies."

Alexis growled. "Do *not* give Eve ideas!"

She whirled around and released a barrage of hardened energy charges. "We need backup. Call SI Torrence."

No need, a soft female voice cut in. *I am here.*

"Gemini!" the twins cried in unison.

Are we glad to hear from you, Alexis told the AI. *Can you do something about that ship before we're overrun?*

Already on it, Gemini replied. *I tried a warning shot, but they obviously didn't take me seriously.*

Gemini dropped her ship's cloaking as she swooped in over the park. Her words were accompanied by another explosion, this one much larger than the first.

The enemy ship listed crazily as a series of explosions came from inside.

All you have to know is where the weak point is, she sang as she loosed a spread of missiles to take out the enemy mechs. *Dumbasses must have never seen* Star Wars *since they left their vents unprotected.*

Alexis supposed it was only right an alien species would have missed out on the Earth classic. Still, it felt a little bit too easy. Her suspicions were confirmed when the ship quit listing altogether and started a slow plummet toward the ground—right where the unit's mechs were standing.

CHAPTER ELEVEN

"Get out of here!" Alexis yelled over the comm as she sprinted toward the ship without any idea what she was going to do to regain control of the situation. "We messed up!"

Gabriel was by her side, no clearer than his sister about how they were going to avoid getting smooshed by the ship whose diameter covered most of the park. "Don't they care that they're going to kill what troops they have left down here?"

"They're *programs*," Alexis panted. "They don't care about anything."

Trey felt sudden calmness descend at the realization they wouldn't clear the park in time. "This is just like in the movies, except there's usually nobody beneath the damned ship when it crashes."

Alexis tuned out K'aia's bitching, her mind whirling with options she rapidly discarded for saving them from repeating the battle. "I do not want to go through all this

NR ROBERTS & MICHAEL ANDERLE

again," she declared, drawing on the Etheric harder than she'd ever dared to do before.

"I'm not arguing," Gabriel told her. "Just don't burn yourself out, okay?"

Alexis didn't have time to think about the possibility. She grabbed Gabriel's hand and continued to pull energy as they ran, vaulting the downed Ookens without a thought.

The ship continued to drop, falling so slowly Alexis figured at least something inside it was still working to keep it afloat. Still, she thought it was picking up speed, or it could have been a trick of perception played by her mind as they neared the ruined gardens at the front of the park.

Time slowed further as they entered the shadow of the ship and Alexis realized that they had to act now or lose the scenario and remain in the game for another six months.

Spurred by her refusal to repeat her actions of earlier in the day, she let go of Gabriel's hand and raised her arms as if she were going to hold up the ship by sheer force of will.

She released the Etheric energy she'd hoarded while running. It blazed out from her hands and the crown of her head and shot upward in a thick stream so bright it hurt Gabriel's eyes.

Gabriel recovered just in time to see a surviving Ooken lunge for Alexis. He skipped through the Etheric and came out in between Alexis and her attacker.

The Ooken didn't appear to care that its target had changed. It ground to a halt and whipped its back tentacles at Gabriel, readying the rifle in its clawed hands.

Gabriel kept his cool and released a barrage of Etheric

energy shaped like needles. He darted in as the needles tore into the Ooken's naked body.

The Ooken toppled but caught itself with its tentacles. It screeched at Gabriel and lunged again, murder in its cold, black eyes.

Gabriel was ready. He manifested a sword and shield out of Etheric energy and blocked the attack, taking off the tips of two tentacles with a sweep of the crackling blade. He wheeled around and blasted another Ooken with a stream of cold fire.

The pale blue energy left ashes where the Ooken had been winding up to attack. It also drew the attention of yet more Ookens.

Gabriel moved faster than the unenhanced eye could see, his only thought to keep Alexis safe while she worked to save them all. His sword flashed bright loops in the darkness as he ducked and darted through the soon-to-be-dead enemy soldiers.

Alexis was only vaguely aware of Gabriel's fight. Her entire concentration was on the sinking behemoth above and how in seven hells she was going to keep it from crushing everyone in the park.

She saw the civilians trapped in the building and her teammates who were going to die along with them if she allowed the ship to crash. The responsibility lay with her and Gabriel to ensure their survival. Alexis understood her parents implicitly at that moment. Why they were the first to act whenever injustice reared its ugly head.

She gritted her teeth and poured energy into the beam. The ship rained molten metal where the energy ripped into it. Fire fell all around, setting the park alight.

It wasn't enough.

The ship was still on its deadly course despite Alexis pushing it. She gathered herself, realizing that brute force was only going to get her so far.

She had to fight smarter.

There's no freaking way we're letting this go down, she told Gabriel. *I'm going to try something different.*

I've got you, Gabriel promised. *Just don't fight fair, you got me?*

Alexis flashed a grin. *Never intended to.*

Devon, Vid-doc Vault

Eve dialed time in the game down to a standstill and opened an audio link. "Bethany Anne, Michael, it is time."

"Already?" Michael asked with skepticism.

Eve pressed her lips together. "They're about to unlock their peak abilities, so I paused the program and called. You did ask to be informed when they looked to be reaching this point."

"We're on our way," Bethany Anne told Eve. "Disable the nanocurtain."

A few moments later, Bethany Anne and Michael walked out of the Etheric.

"Put the curtain back up," Bethany Anne instructed as she crossed to the viewing area.

Michael took his seat in the viewing area, his attention fixed on the screen and the carnage that was paused there. "I thought it would be a bit longer before they were ready to face Ookens."

"What can I say?" Eve asked. "Trey was done by the end

of the second stint in 'stasis,' and K'aia only had a few tweaks. The rest was always going to depend on when Alexis and Gabriel reached emotional maturity and found it within themselves to unlock their full potential."

Bethany Anne narrowed her eyes, unable to fully repress her reaction to the sight of her children neck-deep in what could easily be mistaken for the climactic scene from one of those movies that made back its exorbitant production budget so many times over that they flogged the story to death with sequels that never matched the passion of the original.

She indicated the screen with a finger. "Catch us up. What led to this, and what else does the program intend to put my children through?"

Eve's eyes flickered while she ran through the milestones the children had passed. "The final step is the one that mattered, the one that unlocked the endgame."

Bethany Anne fixed Eve with the look only a mother can give. "You're prevaricating."

Eve had the grace to blush, no mean feat for an android. "I don't want to proceed with what the program is suggesting," she admitted.

That drew Michael's attention. "What exactly is it suggesting that is making you so reticent?" he inquired.

Eve hesitated before answering. "Breaking their connection to each other. The program has identified that as a potential weakness if one of them dies in battle."

"No." Bethany Anne stated, her eyes flaring red as the unthinkable thought wormed its way into her head. "There's no need for that because they're not ever going to be put in that situation."

"Bethany Anne, it's a simulation." Michael ignored the shaking of the vault, just like he ignored the energy pouring from his wife. He took her hand, keeping his voice low and calm. "Get control of yourself before you cause an earthquake."

The energy receded as she clamped down on it, but Bethany Anne felt no peace. She glared at Michael, her eyes still bright with red light. "I don't care if it's a simulation. I won't have my babies suffer."

Michael pointed at the screen. "Look at them," he demanded. "They are not babies. They are adults. No matter what our perception of their lives, theirs is different. They've lived those years with and without us, and earned the right to put themselves in whatever situations they wish to."

He brought his hand back to clasp hers. "Did you think they would stay with us?" he asked gently. "They are our children, made from us. They have the entire universe at their feet. Would *you* stay?"

Bethany Anne bowed her head, knowing Michael was right. Why did he have to be? The vision she'd had of the four of them remaining together slipped away and was replaced by the reality that Alexis and Gabriel were highly-trained fighters. "No, I guess I knew they would want to spread their wings," she admitted.

"We need them in this war," Michael reminded her. "They're every bit as powerful as we are."

Bethany Anne pulled her hand free and turned away, regretting it when she faced the screen and saw the proof of what Michael was saying. "I can't look at our children as assets, Michael."

"That's why you had the *Gemini* built," Michael soothed. "And that's why we're going to allow the program to run."

Bethany Anne still hesitated.

"If they don't get the inoculation," he continued, "what would be the chances of survival of anyone around them if it comes to the worst?"

Bethany Anne hated it on the rare occasions she had to concede that Michael was right. However, she knew her children as well as she knew herself and had to accept that the best way to protect Alexis and Gabriel—as well as the others—in the long term was to allow them to be hurt right now while they were contained within the Vid-doc system.

"Fine. Run the program," she told Eve.

"As you wish," Eve replied.

"I *don't* fucking wish," Bethany Anne ground out. "But better here where I can pull them out if it goes too far."

The innards of the ship were twisting under the twin pressures of gravity and Alexis' pushback. Alexis continued to push with the beam and opened her awareness to take in the structure of the ship as the energy passed through the grinding metal.

Alexis strained to contain the whirlwind in her mind. Knowledge met instinct, and the collision tore her into infinite pieces. She was on the ground and in the air. She was human and ship, air and energy and lightning all at once, with no beginning and no end. She had no body, yet she was embodied in every atom in existence.

She was no longer in a game. She was part of the ship, and the ship was part of her.

She could taste the elements that made up the hull, metallic like blood. Perhaps she was bleeding from somewhere, but she couldn't tell when she was made only from Etheric energy and the determination not to lose.

Everything was connected, and Alexis became certain her will was the ultimate state of being. On the heels of that revelation came the knowledge that she no longer needed a body to contain her mind. She shed the awkward encumbrance as the thought came to her, and she suddenly realized something. She'd known all along that matter was something her brain *perceived* as real. If she had been transfigured this way, she could also change the ship.

Gabriel gasped when Alexis vanished in a blaze of light that streaked upward and enveloped the ship. The distraction allowed his opponent to get its tentacles around his body. He Mysted out of the Ooken's grip, crying out across the mindspace for his sister.

He felt she was there, but he was unable to connect with her.

Then, even that was gone.

The disconnect broke him. Whatever Alexis had done had separated him from her for the first time in his life. Gabriel dropped to his knees as though someone had cut his strings. His mind screamed that he'd been cut off from some vital part of himself, and he was flooded with grief for the loss.

The Ookens swarmed him, tearing at his armor ineffectively. Their weight bore down, crushing his body.

Gabriel didn't care. Alexis was gone, and he didn't want to live in a world where she wasn't there.

The weight on him grew unbearable, but he didn't notice. The darkness fitted the landscape of his heart. Alarms in his armor were nothing but background noise compared to the overwhelming pain of loss his mind could only process as a wordless scream. Even the pain became unimportant. Without Alexis, he had no purpose.

No reason to fight.

No reason to live.

The weight suddenly lifted, and the light returned to rake his eyes. He looked up dazedly into K'aia's stern face and blinked away tears.

"You don't get to check out that easy," K'aia admonished as she pulled him to his feet.

Gabriel blinked again, raising a hand to shield his eyes from the lancing torchlight coming from K'aia's helmet. Something wasn't right about the situation. His mind cleared when he realized what it was. "You can't be down here," he whispered. "Get back in your mech."

K'aia still had him by the arm. She shook him roughly, thinking the action might rattle his brain and restore sense. "What, and let you give up? Not a damn chance. We've lost Alexis, and there's no way I'm losing you, too. Now get up and *fight!*"

Gabriel realized he was surrounded by the unit. They had abandoned their mechs, and all were fighting to keep the Ookens from him while he was vulnerable.

Trey... Trey was covered in wounds and taking more as fast as his nanocytes could heal them. Boden had lost his wings. They hung tattered down his back. Sibil bled freely from the stump of her tail, while Gorrak could only kneel and keep fighting.

He uttered a cry of despair when he saw Pootie lying still with charred dead Ookens scattered around her like the petals of a macabre flower, arranged by the force of the blast that she took them out with.

It was enough to break his heart all over again.

Gabriel was filled with an emotion he couldn't name. It was so clean and cold it washed away his grief and brought with it a righteous fury. What he'd lost was more than he was willing to give, and he was done with being taken from. He felt for the Etheric and opened it. His feet left the ground as he drew hard and fast, becoming a conduit for the energy.

K'aia took a step back, suddenly afraid as the sweet boy she knew was transformed into a red-eyed monster lacking a single shred of pity or remorse.

Gabriel lifted a hand and pointed at the Ookens attacking Trey. "DIE," he told them in a voice that shook the earth.

The Ookens obeyed.

CHAPTER TWELVE

Alexis.

Who was Alexis?

She was pure thought, a ghost, a myth. She was…free.

No, she told herself. *I am Alexis. I am human, and I have a job to do.*

With her acceptance of self came an awareness of having been torn asunder. A vital part of her had been taken. All this passed in a fraction of a second, and in the next second, she remembered what was missing.

Where was Gabriel?

She searched the mindspace and came up empty. More than empty. She'd been gutted, despite having no guts to rip out. Half of her whole was gone. Had she made this happen? Had she shucked her connection to Gabriel when she'd abandoned her corporeal attachment?

Guilt wracked her, adding to the cyclone of emotional disorientation she was in danger of being sucked into. The frightening thought that Gabriel had been killed ate at her, superseding her guilt. Blind panic was replaced by anger.

Alexis felt her being pulse with the urge to destroy whatever had taken her brother.

The Seven. They would die burning from the inside out.

Before she could disengage from the ship, something pulled at the edge of her awareness. There was someone—no, some*ones*—drawing on the energy she was suspended in.

Living beings below. Without eyes, she saw them fighting, knots of vibrant energy. Gabriel was the brightest. Trey and K'aia were somewhat muted since they weren't actively drawing on the Etheric, but they were unmistakable.

Her inspection showed her that Gabriel was unharmed, unlike the Ookens whose twisted energy he was snuffing out. Even the civilians cowering in safety carried a ghost flame, the touch of energy that signified life.

Alexis was flooded with relief and a renewed sense of purpose. She had a ship to take care of.

She flowed around the hull and raised the ship, halting its downward progress. Next, she insinuated herself in the spaces between atoms, breaking the bonds that formed the compounds.

The ship ceased to be as she scattered it to the winds. Alexis felt her consciousness expand as her exploration of matter manipulation blossomed into true understanding. The physics of the universe meant nothing to her. Everything she'd learned before this moment was only supposition made by people who had never been connected to the fabric of reality like she was right now. Her knowledge grew as she experimented, and the rapidity with which it happened intoxicated her.

Time itself—

Alexis. Enough.

Whose voice was that? Someone who must be obeyed; that she knew. Alexis thought briefly about ignoring the command, but something deep in her psyche told her disobedience was not an option.

Then she would fight.

But wait, why would she fight? What was she fighting for?

Your brother, her mother reminded her.

The sense of being cut off from something vital returned to Alexis, dragging her down from the high she'd almost given in to.

Gabriel. I almost forgot myself completely.

Bethany Anne spoke quietly in a tone Alexis had never heard from her mother before. **It's tempting to give yourself up to peace. It would be a relief some days. But you don't have that option, my love. None of us do. We have to be the barrier, the line the assholes don't dare cross. Duty doesn't care how tired you are. Evil never sleeps.**

"I'm sorry," she whispered from lips she'd reformed.

Alexis looked around and saw the carnage the invasion had wreaked on the city. She looked down and saw Gabriel, and their bond was restored.

I thought I'd lost you for a minute, Gabriel told her in their mindspace.

Only for a minute? Alexis replied. *I almost lost myself forever.*

She increased her mass to normal levels and came

down to land beside Gabriel. "We belong together. Let's not do the separation thing again too soon, yeah?"

Gabriel's eyes shone. He threw his arms around Alexis, and they stood that way for a long moment without saying a word.

Trey cleared his throat. "If we're all done with the reunion? They're getting away."

Alexis wondered what he meant since she'd made certain that the ship wasn't taking anyone anywhere. Then she saw the second, much smaller ship breaking the planet's atmosphere. "Gemini!"

I'm here, the AI replied as she brought the ship down to the ground and dropped the ramp. *Get aboard quickly.*

Gabriel paused to pick up Pootie's unnaturally still form in one arm and slung the other around Jentek, while Trey and Sibil supported Gorrak. Boden limped up the ramp behind Alexis with K'aia's assistance, and Sibil made it under her own power.

Gabriel took one look at the sorry bunch once the ramp had lifted and sent the injured to the infirmary for Pod-doc treatment.

"I'll take Pootie," Sibil offered.

"It's too late for her," Gabriel told her sadly.

Sibil nodded, her eyes shining. "Yeah, but she went out with a bang, protecting people who couldn't take care of themselves."

Gabriel handed Pootie over reluctantly. "You're right."

Alexis put her hand on Gabriel's shoulder. "That's all any of us can hope for."

The twins parted from the rest of the unit and headed for the bridge at a run as the *Gemini* broke the atmosphere.

Gemini was waiting for them when they arrived. "Strap yourselves in. This is going to get a little bumpy."

Alexis took her chair with an incredulous look. "Really?"

Gemini winked at her. "No, not really. It just sounded better than 'We're going to have perfectly smooth transit, so seatbelts are unnecessary.'"

Gabriel looked askance at the AI. "Riiight. Where did they go?"

Gemini split the viewscreen so they retained the view of beyond the ship while still having a map of the system. "They, who? If you are referring to your crew, they are in the infirmary receiving treatment for their injuries. If you meant the Kurtherian ship, it shot off toward the outer limits. They have a head start, but we are going to catch them in thirty-nine min— Oh. You have an incoming call."

"Onscreen, please," Gabriel instructed.

The map was replaced by the face of an apoplectic Yollin. "What is this?" SI Torrence demanded. "Where in the galaxy did you get that ship, and why is your unit heading straight for the front line without orders?"

Alexis disengaged from the *Gemini's* navigation system and offered him a small smile. "I'm sorry. We appreciate everything you've done for us, but we've decided to part ways with the military. We can end this war if we're not bound by procedure."

We did? Gabriel asked.

Alexis lifted a shoulder. *Sure. Unless you want to go line up and be shot down with the other ships?*

Fair point, Gabriel conceded. He gave SI Torrence the

same determined smile. "We're going to get to the heart of this."

"You're going to get yourselves killed!" SI Torrence exclaimed hotly.

"It's a very real possibility," Alexis agreed calmly. "But we'll be taking out Kurtherian command at the same time, so…" She shrugged, leaving the rest unspoken and giving their former instructor a moment to put the pieces together.

"You're going to be the death of me," Torrence grumbled. "And I don't mean figuratively. But if anyone can back up such preposterous claims, it's you two." He bent at the console he was using, and the twins received a deluge of data. "I just gave you all the classified information about Kurtherian command I could access. Good luck, and please make it worth the punishment I'm going to get for assisting you in your mutiny."

The twins felt for their Yollin guide. They both knew the penalty for mutiny was death. "We'll make it so your name goes down as the Yollin who turned the tide against the Kurtherians," Alexis promised.

"Yeah," Gabriel agreed. "But there won't be any Kurtherians left to tell the tale. We'll make sure Gemini gets the video to Command."

Gemini signed Torrence off at a wave from Alexis, leaving her and Gabriel to make their plans.

"Do you really think going rogue is the best idea?" Gabriel asked.

"Do you doubt we can beat this game?" Alexis asked in return.

"Honestly? I'm not thinking of it as a game. I haven't

been for a while now, but it's my place to think of the consequences when you tear off on one of your ideas, no matter which world we're living in." Gabriel opened the first of the files they'd been sent. "There's a lot of information here."

"That's why you have me," Gemini told him. "Give me a minute to sort through it for relevance."

She came back fifty-one seconds later with a wide, almost predatory grin. "I believe I have located the Seven's base of operations."

"Show us," Alexis told her.

Gemini returned the map to the viewscreen and zeroed in on the not-so-empty-space between two, no, three star systems, set back from the battle zones.

"This system has nothing that should have attracted their attention," Gemini informed them. "Yet there are significant defenses around the battlestation."

Alexis tilted her head. "We know it's a battlestation because?"

"I helped myself to the database of the ship you dematerialized," Gemini replied airily. "Well, what I could get to before you destroyed it."

Alexis didn't need an invitation to dig into the goodies Gemini had procured. Her eyes flickered as she scanned the information. "Good work. Now tell me…"

Gabriel did his best not to zone out as Alexis questioned Gemini in rapid yet excruciating detail and formulated their plan of attack on the battlestation's outer defenses. He got the part about phishing to get access to the system but lost her when she started throwing around words like "Heartbleed" and "Stuxnet." It was one thing to know this stuff, which he did in theory, but it was another entirely to understand it like Alexis did.

Gabriel studied the schematic of the battlestation. Not for the first time, he found himself wishing he'd done more than retain information so he could pass tests and get out onto the training field. Maybe if he'd had put as much effort into understanding what he'd been taught as he had into soaking up tactical knowledge, he wouldn't be sitting by while Alexis did all the mental heavy-lifting on the technical side of things.

Then again…

Gabriel let go of his doubts. Teamwork meant everyone contributed their talents and skills. Nobody ever won by wishing they were someone else. He spotted something that struck him as anomalous until he applied the context of his knowledge. How many times had TOM told them he'd been humbled by their mother's course of action while recounting stories of the years before he and Alexis were born? He'd always suspected there was a certain arrogance to Kurtherians in general, but this proved it without a doubt.

"I don't know," Alexis told Gemini. "It could be that it's so out of date we could sneak it in." She felt Gabriel's attention wander and read the distracted look he wore for what it was. "What are you seeing?" she asked him.

"Wait, go back a bit," he told her, pushing his hair out of his eyes as he sat back from his console. "You lost me just after you and Gemini started talking about phishing attacks."

Alexis waved a hand. "Forget that. We were rehashing ancient history. Figuring out how to get past the defense systems is my job. Yours is to identify the weak spots in the battlestation. How do we take it down when we get in?"

Gabriel studied the schematic closely. *This* he got. "Okay, so we have two options. Both mean us going aboard and getting to the center of the station without getting caught."

"Doesn't sound like there's much of a choice," Alexis countered.

"Course there is," Gabriel told her. "Inner security is almost nonexistent," he told her. "It's like they don't believe anyone could get past the outer defenses."

Alexis snorted. "Seriously?"

Gabriel shrugged. "I'm sure there are guards, but tech? Nothing like what we're used to." He highlighted the reactor core chamber. "See?"

Alexis pressed her lips together. "So all we have to do is make it there and we're golden?"

Gabriel hesitated to confirm without having a visual. "All I'm saying is that there are no generators for nanocurtain tech. No inner Gates. I don't think any of the measures we were expecting exist in this timeline. Anything else we've got, right?"

He waited for Alexis to reply but continued when she just waved. "Okay, so say you do your thing and get us inside. My thinking is that we make our way to the reactor room and set off an explosion that can be seen from the Empire."

Alexis liked the idea. "Just one thing. How do you expect to blow it up?"

Gabriel grinned. "I was *kinda* listening when you and Gemini were talking. How difficult would it be to launch a digital attack on them as a distraction for the physical one?"

Alexis matched her brother's smile. "I see where you're going with this. I have something in mind that would work, providing I can rewrite it. While the Kurtherians and their minions are running around trying to stop their computer systems from tearing themselves to pieces, we plant explosives as the icing on the exploding cake."

"You've got it," Gabriel enthused, twisting in his seat to face Alexis. "Option one, we blow the reactor with timed charges. Option two, we set remote-activated charges."

Alexis folded her arms, seeing a flaw in his plan. "What if we don't get off the station in time? Or the Kurtherians find a way to block the detonation signal? I don't think we should risk either of those." She shuddered. "Ugh. Why am I the voice of reason all of a sudden?"

Gabriel fixed Alexis with a knowing look. He didn't have to be a mind reader to know that his sister had come down with a severe case of nobility. "How is what you're about to suggest in any way reasonable?"

"It's just a game," she reminded him. "It's not like we're going to die for real if we tear just a *small* rift."

Gabriel stood firm. "That's where you're wrong. I get that you want to take the easy way out now, but how will that affect us one day in the future?" He furrowed his brow as his thought came to him fully-formed. "We could learn something here that will save us in the future. Sure, it's a game, but it's also our testing ground."

Alexis opened her mouth to speak, but Gabriel wasn't done.

He spread his arms to encompass the entire gameworld.

"How much of our lives have we lived in this safety net? Living without consequences? You realize that net will be taken away forever once we leave here?" He met Alexis' dark gaze. "We'll never have the luxury of it being 'just a game' again."

Alexis lowered her eyes. "That was what you meant when you said you hadn't been thinking of this as a game."

"Finally." Gabriel closed his eyes and shook his head. Now wasn't the time to pay his sister back for all the times she'd ragged on him for being slower to reach a conclusion. That was childhood, and they weren't children anymore. He took Alexis' face in his hands and touched his forehead to hers. "I know it's scary. We have to run a real risk, and we just lost our explosives expert. Would you open a rift in the real world?"

Alexis pulled free and crossed her arms, tilting her chin to an obstinate angle. "In the right circumstance? Yeah."

Gabriel was taken aback. "For real? After what the rift did to Qu'Baka?"

Alexis nodded. "*Because* of what the rift did to Qu'Baka, and because of what we lost. Aunt Addix would be the first to tell me to be true to myself. Well, I'm going to find the Kurtherian who opened that rift, and before I throw them into a rift *I* made, I'm going to enjoy every minute of destroying whatever it is they hold dear. To do that, I need to be in control."

"I miss Aunt Addix, too," Gabriel murmured. He sat back and folded his hands in his lap. "I'm all for your plan. It goes beyond my instinct to protect you from harm. I had an epiphany when we were separated. Wait, I can share it."

He closed his eyes and thought back to the inexplicable moment.

Alexis gasped. "Yes! That's exactly it!" She leaned forward and grabbed Gabriel's hands. "Just get me to the core. I can do this. A rift the size of my pinkie nail, and bye-bye battlestation."

"You can keep it contained until we're back on the *Gemini?*" he asked.

Alexis let go and lifted her hands. "We'll do it together, or we'll keep trying until we get it. You're right; we aren't playing anymore. We might not be able to really die here, but that's an advantage we can use. If we fluff it, we keep trying until we succeed. We should tell K'aia and Trey what we're planning to do."

Gabriel raised an eyebrow. "Do we have to? You know K'aia's not going to like it."

Alexis giggled, slapped Gabriel's arm, and turned back to her console. "Ass. I have a multilayered attack to write. *You* just volunteered to tell the others what's going down."

CHAPTER THIRTEEN

Open Space, QBS *Gemini*, Bridge

K'aia wished that she'd gone with the twins to the bridge when they boarded the ship instead of assisting the rest of the unit to the infirmary. Perhaps if she had, she would have been there to intercede when the twins lost their damned minds. "No. Just no. I categorically forbid it, and *no*."

She stamped her back feet, looking at Trey for support. "For a start, opening a rift is impossible. B, you could be killed attempting it. Three, I don't think any of us wants to get stuck repeating the last few months."

Trey shrugged. "I can see it working, as long as Gemini and Alexis can get us in."

"There's no *way* we're in the same scenario," Gabriel replied. "You know how it works. We complete an event and move on to the next. If we reset—which is *so* not going to happen—we'll reset to the decision to chase the Kurtherian ship. If I'm wrong and we get set back to

Zenith Station, Alexis will do every bit of your coursework."

"Hey!" Alexis called.

"It's your theory, "Gabriel reminded her.

Alexis lifted a shoulder, continuing to type without breaking her flow. "Whatever. It's not like I'm going to have to do it."

K'aia huffed. "You're going to go ahead no matter what I say, aren't you?"

Alexis looked up momentarily from her keyboard to flash a grin at K'aia. "Anyone would think you know us."

K'aia tipped her head back and sighed, then walked to her station and sat heavily with another drawn-out sigh. "Fine. Tell us what craziness you're dragging us into this time."

Gabriel broke it down for them. "The short version is that Alexis and Gemini are going to trick the battlestation the Kurtherians are using as their command center into thinking we're actually the ship we're chasing, and vice-versa. They'll blow up their own ship, thinking that's the invader. Then the four of us sneak in, make our way to the reactor room, do our thing, and get the hell out of there before the place goes *boom*. Sound good to you?"

"What about the rest of the unit?" K'aia asked.

"Are any of them fit to fight if we run into trouble?" Gabriel countered.

"Well, no," K'aia told him.

"Then it's just us and the Kurtherians," Gabriel told her. "Get ready for a rough transfer. It's not going to be a picnic getting your armor through the Etheric."

Trey cracked his knuckles and headed for the weapons locker where he'd left his staff. "Bring on the madness."

Gemini reappeared, interrupting K'aia's groan. "The Kurtherian ship has slowed considerably, and I have finished copying myself to the intercept drone."

Alexis emitted a squeak and doubled over her keyboard. "No time for talking. I'm up."

Her world shrank to the keyboard and Gemini's voice in her mind. She released the drone she'd had Gemini copy the relevant parts of herself to and watched with her teeth pressing grooves into her bottom lip as it sped across the void to intercept the ship's communication with the battlestation.

The Gemini in the drone reported back to the whole Gemini that her task was complete. Gemini passed the link to Alexis, who got to work identifying the blocks of alien symbols that had been used as permissions and feeding them to the AI.

Gabriel vowed to do better at learning Kurtherian programming languages when this was over. He ignored the muttered curses from his sister as he watched over her shoulder. That was his clue that she was entirely immersed in her task. Normally his interest would be met with a complaint that she couldn't think to type when he was watching and the demand that he go watch on his own screen.

Gemini had thoughtfully provided a view of the battlestation. Gabriel resisted the urge to celebrate when a bright beam came from the battlestation and disintegrated the Kurtherian ship instead of theirs. "We good?"

"We're in," Alexis announced, pausing to wipe the sweat from her forehead. "Now for the tricky part."

"She's going to take control of their systems and have them all freak out," Gabriel explained for K'aia's and Trey's benefit.

"Not if you're not quiet!" Alexis snapped. "Gemini, keep messing with their sensors and cloak before someone looks out and sees us. It would be just our luck. I don't want them getting a visual and figuring out we're not who we say we are before we get aboard."

Silence reigned over the bridge, broken only by the sharp clicking of Alexis' keyboard suffering horrific abuse at her fingertips.

Everyone jumped nearly out of their skin—or carapace, in K'aia's case—when she suddenly thrust her chair back and leapt to her feet.

"What are you waiting for?" she asked. "Let's go already!"

She grabbed Trey's free hand and took him into the Etheric. Gabriel emerged beside her with K'aia in the next instant. Their journey was short but hard on the twins.

They emerged in a niche in an empty corridor a few moments later, K'aia and Trey with their guards up while the twins took a moment to recover from the exertion and replenish their energy levels.

Trey glanced at the corridor beyond with a distinct feeling of "meh."

"Not impressed?" K'aia asked.

"It's so…ordinary," Trey explained, indicating the utilitarian grays the corridor was appointed in. "I thought we'd see some of the cool crystal structures like in the factory vids."

"The lack of them just means there's no Ookens here," Gabriel told him. "That's something to be thankful for."

"Which way?" Alexis asked Gabriel, counting down the seconds until stage two of her digital attack was in full effect.

The lights flickered, drawing a soft snicker from Alexis. "Okay, the cameras are down. We can move."

Gabriel checked the map he'd downloaded to his internal HUD and pointed the way. "We go up three levels. There's an access shaft on that deck that takes us down to the engineering deck. From there, it's a straight shot to the reactor room, as long as we don't run into any trouble."

"Would a little trouble be the worst thing?" Trey asked with a mischievous grin as they made their way along the corridor after Gabriel.

K'aia slapped the back of his head. "Damn right, it would. We want to get in and out without them knowing we're here."

Trey rubbed the sore spot with his free hand. "Says you. A little pew-pew goes a long way."

Alexis raised an eyebrow. "What does that even mean?"

Trey sighed. "It means this is going to be a pretty boring mission if all we're doing is sneaking around."

"Just wait," Gabriel promised. "I can guarantee we'll run into something *riiiight* when it's vital that we don't. There's a law, you know?"

"I'm not sure Murphy's law applies here," Alexis countered.

"You're kidding, right?" Gabriel argued. "You know,

Uncle Scott once told me that he reckons one day scientists will figure out that it's a universal constant. Whatever can go wrong, will."

He heard footsteps in the near-distance and ducked into a recess near the intersection of the corridor, motioning for the others to do the same.

They waited nervously as the footsteps got closer. A pair of armored Kurtherians with their helmets deactivated clomped through the intersection, unaware of the four interlopers pressing themselves out of sight in the tight space.

"And you thought this was a good idea," K'aia grumbled after the Kurtherians passed out of hearing.

"It is!" Alexis whispered.

Gabriel indicated a door on the other side of the intersection. "The stairs through there take us up, but we'll have to be careful."

Getting up the stairs went without incident, as did getting to the hatch they were aiming for. It was only when they were about to climb inside the maintenance shaft that they ran into a problem.

Alexis was the first to get eyes on the bots. "Dammit, there's hundreds of them!"

"Can't you deactivate them?" K'aia asked, uncertain she wanted to get into the shaft with robots bearing power tool appendages.

Alexis shook her head. "Take a look. There's no pattern to their movements. They're not being controlled by any system."

K'aia could have told that from the way many of them were spinning on the spot without releasing whatever mechanism kept them adhered to the vertical shaft. "Then we'll have to find another route because there's no way my epitaph is going to read 'killed by insane maintenance bots who thought she was a faulty processor.'"

Gabriel snickered. "It won't come to that. Alexis, you say they're not connected to any network? Does that mean we can destroy them without alerting anyone to our location?"

Alexis shrugged. "Sure, but what we *can't* do is let off a bunch of Etheric energy to do it."

Trey leaned into the shaft with his staff at the ready. "I can take care of this." He loosed a low charge that coated the shaft in baleful red light, and the bots fell away from the interior, to the relief of them all.

They watched them rain down the shaft and waited to see if there was any response. Gabriel decided they hadn't triggered a high alert, probably because Alexis' and Gemini's attack had everyone tied up elsewhere.

"Anything on the system?" he asked Alexis.

Her eyes unfocused while she communicated with Gemini. "No," she told him, confirming his suspicion.

"Great." Gabriel gave the order to move, and they followed him onto the ladder one at a time.

K'aia grumbled something about the unfairness of a world designed for the two-legged as she descended.

"Could be worse," Trey consoled. "There could be a shitload of armed guards after us again."

"Don't tempt fate," Alexis warned. "And by fate, I mean Eve."

Gabriel wasn't so sure Eve was still making additions to the game. Their situation felt too severe and lacked the unexpected twists they had experienced previously for him to think it had been tweaked by her hand. He led the team down the seemingly endless shaft, keeping his mind clear and his attention on the map.

He slowed as they passed an access hatch, behind which they could hear frantic activity. "Your attack?" he asked, looking up at Alexis.

Alexis winked. "You know it. I designed a gift that keeps on giving. The more attempts they make to dig it out, the more times it replicates. The more they vary their counter-attacks, the more my little program learns and evolves. I expect it's gotten quite large by now. We should start noticing—"

The shaft, and therefore everything in and around the shaft, lurched.

Alexis would have clapped with delight if she hadn't been clinging to the ladder in an attempt to avoid being thrown off it. "We should hurry," she told the others. "Engage your helmets. Things are about to get nasty in the life support systems."

K'aia touched the button on her armor's collar to activate her helmet. "If you can mess things up that badly, why couldn't you have the battlestation blow itself up? I would have been happy to provide the popcorn."

Alexis sighed. "If only it was that easy. Eventually, the Kurtherians will find a way to stop my attack, and they'll regain control of their systems. My guess is that we'll get to the reactor room and find all of their engineers working to reverse the damage to the core."

"That's when we'll throw them a curveball," Gabriel enthused.

"You mean, that's when we finally get to do something useful," Trey put in with feeling. He paused to shift the weight of his staff.

"Watch where you're pointing that thing!" K'aia exclaimed when the butt swung dangerously close to her helmet visor.

"Oh, crap. Sorry." Trey shifted the staff again. "Guess I've gotten used to working without it. It's like I have to remember to direct a third leg that doesn't tell me it's in the way."

K'aia snorted. "Try having four legs and a team who thinks it's the peak of hilarity to have you climb a never-ending series of ladders."

"You would see it that way," Alexis told her amusedly.

"We're getting close to our exit," Gabriel assured her. "Only eight more decks."

"Only eight?" K'aia repeated flatly. "Yaaay."

Trey picked up his thought again when he was sure he wasn't about to brain K'aia by accident. "I mean, wiping out the Ookens was fun and all, but it can't replace the thrill of close combat with someone who's intelligent enough to think about more than the urge to eat my face."

"Empress forbid that happens," K'aia continued in the same snarky tone. "You're far too pretty to end up a snack for an Ooken."

"Don't I know it," Trey agreed amiably.

"Besides," Gabriel added dryly, "what would we do without your sparkling commentary on these missions?"

Alexis had too many balls in the air to join in the shit talk. Apart from keeping track of her physical actions, she was fighting off a number of Kurtherians who were getting ever closer to locking her and Gemini out of the battlestation's systems.

We just got locked out of secondary life support, Gemini informed her.

We'd better not lose primary, then, Alexis replied. *Do what you can. I have to concentrate on the numbers.*

The numbers in question were the equations she was inventing as she went to figure out how to open the microscopic rift she wanted *without* tearing a huge-ass hole in reality she couldn't handle afterward. She'd had no opportunity to learn about the rift her parents had experienced at Qu'Baka since her mother had been preoccupied with arranging a funeral and making arrangements for the influx of Bakas to talk about her experience in the short time they'd exited the game after the event.

There was the added pressure of her wanting to get this right the first time since she had an inkling the game would have learned from everything they'd done this time around if they got killed and reset. There was a chance that nothing they'd done this time would work on the next go-round.

Her HUD was struggling to run at the speed of her thoughts while Gemini was borrowing from her memories as a database for context pertaining to intuition, and she was getting frustrated with the lag in her internal computing speed. *Gemini, can you operate independently for a few minutes? Maintain a connection, but back out of my neural chip so it can run fast enough for me to* think.

Gemini receded, and Alexis had what she needed to concentrate. She tuned the external input down until her concentration was reduced to hand over hand and *don't* misstep, while the back of her mind whirred.

Gabriel called a halt at the access hatch marked on his map. He left the ladder for the slab of metal jutting out from the hatch and slid the dead bot off it with a push of his foot. With the platform clear, he checked each of the team as they reached the platform. "Alexis, you good?"

Alexis held a finger up without changing her faraway look as she stepped onto the platform. "Shh!"

"You're fine, then," Gabriel remarked dryly. "Trey, K'aia?"

Trey hopped off the ladder, his fist held ready for a bump. "Ready for a fight, that's for sure."

Gabriel bumped fists, then opened his hand to point at Trey. "Have your HUD check your endocrine levels and adjust them if necessary. I want you clear and cool, you get me? Good decisions only."

Trey nodded, realizing he'd been sounding like more than one of his uncles pre-attitude adjustment. "Good choices," he promised. "Doesn't mean I can't be happy about the opportunity to kick some Kurtherian ass."

"We're all happy about *that*," K'aia cut in as she left the ladder with a small jump.

Alexis snapped out of her half-trance. "I've *got* it."

CHAPTER FOURTEEN

"Never doubted you for a moment," K'aia told Alexis. "Which is why I have to make sure you understand what you're messing with."

Alexis shook her head as she opened the Etheric over her palm. "I really don't. There's tried and tested science out there, but it's in the hands of the Kurtherians who opened the real rift. All I could do was haul my ideas together and kick them into shape with a mathematical language I made up as I went along. Now all that's left is to bring it into being with the force of my will."

K'aia saved her arguments. She would have to be blind to miss the strength of Alexis' will. It was in her steady gaze and the set of her jaw. This wasn't the pre-teen she'd first met, nor was she the reckless post-adolescent who was so quick to act before considering the full consequences. This was a woman who had the power to save the day, and she knew it. "You realize we're going to lose our cover?"

"All part of the plan," Gabriel told her with a nod at the hatch. "That opens out, so if we can get them to open it for us, all the better."

K'aia grinned. "Ah, I see where you're going with it. Fair enough. It's been a while since I got a real workout." She got into position by the door, ready to catch it and use it as a weapon.

Gabriel tapped the Etheric and manifested a sword and shield, He and Trey took the other side of the hatch, their weapons at the ready. Gabriel would have preferred Jean Dukes Specials at this moment, but in the absence of the best, he'd rather rely on his skill than a weapon made by a stranger.

Alexis shielded herself and began the operation. She started by weaving Etheric energy into a sphere. She built it from the bottom up, layering the energy to ensure it would hold the components she'd created separate from each other until she and Gabriel had dragged K'aia and Trey through the Etheric to the *Gemini*.

Her actions in the Etheric drew some attention at last. The hatch swung open, removing the need for any efforts to get it open, as per Gabriel's plan.

Unfortunately for the two unhelmeted Kurtherians who rushed out, K'aia hadn't had the opportunity to use her full strength in a while. She slammed the door when they were two paces out, and the pair of them brained themselves on the solid metal hatch.

Trey zapped them with his staff, while Gabriel covered him from the next one who was foolish enough to dash out after the first two were downed.

The third's delayed reaction to Gabriel's sword puncturing his chest cavity made Alexis laugh.

The Kurtherian looked at the glowing blade lodged in his ribs with incomprehension, then collapsed with his mouth stretched in a surprised O when his mind was belatedly informed of the damage that'd been done to his body.

Gabriel pulled his sword free at the same time he smashed his shield into the face of another attacking Kurtherian. This one almost got a return blow in before Gabriel whirled to take his head off with an upward swing.

"Save some for us!" Trey complained.

"Get in here, then," Gabriel invited, moving over a bare inch as the rest of the Kurtherian guards rushed the door. A couple got through, but the rest were jammed in unless they wanted to get hacked to death by Gabriel. All of them recognized the modified tech Trey wielded well enough to be wary of it.

K'aia got a glimpse of panicked-looking science-types rushing around the reactor room as she moved to protect Alexis from the soldiers who'd gotten through. "How long until your weapon is ready?"

"Nearly," Alexis told her distractedly, barely noticing the fight around the outside of her shield. The sphere was almost complete. She had to be extra careful here. If the last part wasn't exactly perfect, they'd all get blown to bits along with the battlestation.

At last, the compartments were built and only the space between atoms was left until Alexis compressed that also. Alexis was working entirely by instinct by this point. She was far beyond the transmutation of the elements. For all she understood of the forces she was manipulating, she might as well have been doing magic. Yet, she would succeed where the alchemists had failed, even if her goal was much more challenging than pulling gold from thin air.

She was playing with the fabric of the universe.

Alexis commanded the energy in the compartments to shift. She gave it no choice but to obey.

Each compartment was filled with a different component that, when combined with the others, would act as the catalyst to spark a rift. Finally, she checked her calculations for the nth time to ensure she'd gotten it right, and that the energy field would collapse at the right moment.

Again, simple, but it was no harder to design something to fail than it would have been for her and Gabriel to close a full-sized rift. Alexis sighed with relief when she completed the last layer without incident.

The fabric of the universe would tear. That was a given.

It just wasn't allowed to happen before *she* was ready.

Gabriel felt more than saw that Alexis had completed her whatever-it-was. There was a noticeable drop in ambient Etheric energy, which told him it was time to unblock the door and clear her path to the reactor core. "Trey, I need a space."

Trey shifted stance at Gabriel's quiet order and used the powered end of his staff to blast the Kurtherians back from the door.

Gabriel slid into the gap, killing two Kurtherians before they'd even realized he'd moved. The others burst into action, discharging their staffs in what they thought was Gabriel's direction.

There was just one problem with that plan. Gabriel wasn't occupying any particular space. He phased in and out, employing the technique he'd come up with as a little kid to copy the way Izanami moved around the ship to compliment the kata he was moving through.

Each brief materialization coincided with the deadly execution of a technique he knew as well as breathing. Each peak was accompanied by a drop in the Kurtherians' morale as another of them fell lifeless to the floor.

It didn't help their cause that a number of them fell to friendly fire.

K'aia folded her arms, her front right foot on the throat of the soldier who'd gone for Alexis. She grunted and snuffed him out with a twist of her ankle. "This is what Addix meant," she murmured, thinking back to the conversation they'd had when Addix had told her she would be obsolete by the time Gabriel was fully trained. "They can't touch him."

She still had her role to fulfill as protector of Alexis, however. There would always be moments like this where the twins were playing to their opposite strengths, and K'aia would be required to be there for one or the other. That was a bodyguard's life—to know where she was most needed and *be* there.

Even when the bodies she was responsible for guarding went into battle.

Especially then.

Alexis walked into the reactor room, cupping the sphere in both hands. She felt K'aia at her back and knew Gabriel and Trey were taking care of any threats up front. All she had to do was introduce the sphere into the reactor core and get the hell out of there before the core stripped the protection off and exposed the components of the catalyst.

She ignored the engineers and stepped over the edge of the walkway around the core. It was nothing to alter her mass so she could walk on the air. Her heart hammered in her chest as she hovered with the delicate sphere. This was the last point where things could go wrong.

The battle raged behind Alexis, but she wasn't paying attention. She let out a long breath, then opened the Etheric and thrust her hands inside. She pushed the sphere out of the Etheric and into the reactor core.

"I did it!" she cried, drawing the attention of everyone in the room.

There wasn't time for anything else. She darted back to solid ground, grabbed K'aia, and flung her into the Etheric. Gabriel and Trey landed in the mist at exactly the same time.

Alexis jumped to her feet and helped K'aia up, then started pulling off the Yollin's armor. "Drop your armor, Trey. We have a couple of minutes, that's all."

Gabriel helped Trey, and the four made the transfer to the bridge of the *Gemini*.

"I'm glad you all made it back in one piece," Gemini announced as they tumbled out of the Etheric.

"Get us out of here!" Alexis yelled. "It's going to blow—"

But there was no explosion, no shockwave to tear the *Gemini* apart. But the battlestation was gone. In its place was a bright, jagged tear in the void, and even that was gone when it suddenly collapsed in on itself and winked out of existence.

Gabriel looked at the unfolding spectacle with amazement. "So," he murmured to Alexis. "Do you want to tell Mom she took care of that rift the hard way, or shall we leave it to Dad?"

The bridge faded to black before Alexis could answer.

Devon, The Hexagon, Vid-doc Vault

Bethany Anne paced the space between the Vid-docs with growing impatience. "How long?" she asked Eve for the third time.

"Neural recalibration can't be rushed," Eve replied with a hint of annoyance.

Michael had just as little patience, but his was coiled tightly, holding him still by the control panel. "It's been three hours."

"Perfectly normal," Eve assured him. "The process has to be completed, or they won't retain everything they've gained in the system."

Bethany Anne stopped pacing and stared at Eve. "They could lose their memories?"

"As well as physical abilities," Eve confirmed.

Only Mahi' kept her calm. She sat with her hand resting in Fi'Eireie's, watching the replays of the battles with rapt attention and a growing smile.

An alert went off and ceased immediately.

"That will be Tabitha," Eve informed Bethany Anne and Michael. "Only she can interfere with the system like that."

"Only me," Tabitha announced over the speakers, confirming Eve's prediction. "Well, me and a couple others."

Eve smirked and turned back to the control panel. "I knew it. We're almost ready here."

"That's what you said an hour ago," Michael reminded her.

"Well, excuse me for thinking an hour wasn't long in human terms," Eve shot back.

Bethany Anne raised an eyebrow when the vault door opened to admit Tabitha, Peter, John, Scott, Darryl, and Eric. Gabrielle pushed through the guys and smiled at Bethany Anne. "We didn't want to miss this."

"Anyone else want to crash my children's return?" Bethany Anne asked.

Tabitha grinned. "Oh, hells, yeah. I didn't think you'd want everyone in the Hexagon down here, though."

"You thought right," Michael told her.

"But you are all welcome," Bethany Anne added. "I can't think of anyone else I'd like to share this moment with."

Eve left the console and glided over to the Vid-docs. "Two minutes."

Bethany Anne forgot her annoyance at the wait when the Vid-docs lit up, signifying that they were about to open.

Inside the Vid-docs, Alexis and Gabriel regained consciousness, followed by K'aia and Trey, who came to a moment later.

All four blinked when the light was restored and they found themselves in the Vid-docs. The lids opened to let them out, and there was a whole crowd waiting to greet them.

Alexis climbed out and darted over to dive into Bethany Anne's waiting arms. "Mom! I missed you!"

Bethany Anne held Alexis close, only letting go with one arm to include Gabriel in the embrace when he joined them. Her heart was full of the completeness she felt holding them in her arms, leaving her momentarily speechless.

"It's so good to see you, Mom," Gabriel murmured into the crook of her neck. "Did you see the end of the scenario?"

They opened their arms again to include Michael, whose voice had a slight quaver when he spoke. "Time is a strange thing," he told his children. "It feels to me like it went as slowly for us as it did for you two."

"We're home," Alexis announced, letting go of her parents so she could hug the rest of their greeting party. "I'm so happy to be back on Devon!"

Bethany Anne pulled K'aia into a hug. "You don't get away so easily," she told her. "You did well in there."

K'aia was sure she was blushing, whether it showed on her carapace or not. "Just doing my duty."

Mahi' gasped when she laid eyes on Trey. "I cannot believe it," she breathed. "You are magnificent, my son."

"Kingly," his father added as the three embraced. "You're a son to make anyone proud, and a warrior our people will sing of for generations to come."

Trey was overcome with emotions. "I missed you,

Mahi'," he managed through his tears. "And I'm looking forward to getting to know you, Father."

Bethany Anne couldn't stop smiling. "This calls for a celebration."

Gabriel grinned. "Where did you hide the Cokes? I know you didn't come down here without any."

Tabitha lifted the lid of a cooler she spotted and laughed. "I'm guessing you're right. Here."

The twins accepted gratefully.

"You know, that's the one thing we missed in there," Alexis told everyone. "If you hadn't stepped down as Empress, Coke wouldn't have made it out of the Empire."

Gabriel nodded. "Yeah. 'S good."

Bethany Anne raised an eyebrow, then dissolved into laughter. "You two are most definitely my children."

"They most definitely have your caffeine addiction," Michael added.

Alexis finished her drink and grabbed another from the cooler. "What we have is *taste*. Now, are we going to just hang around in here all day?"

Bethany Anne rolled her eyes at Alexis' impatience, so like her own. "Well, no. You completed the process just in time."

"In time for what?" Gabriel inquired, seeing the seriousness pass over his mother's face. "Did the Seven attack again?"

"No," Bethany Anne told him. "You've missed a lot while you were in the Vid-docs. We'll tell you about it on the way to the ship."

Alexis' eyes widened as she realized there was a voice missing from her mind. "Gemini!"

"Her ship is berthed on the *Baba Yaga*," Michael assured her.

The conversation continued as the group made their way to the surface. By the time they'd reached the Baba Yaga, the twins knew all about Gödel.

Alexis met Gabriel's gaze with a hard stare. *It's funny. I hadn't expected to know the name of the Kurtherian we're going to destroy. They're usually more...generic. You know?*

Michael's voice cut into their mindspace. *You will leave Gödel to us.*

The twins whirled on Michael. "But, Dad!" Alexis protested. "She owes us for Aunt Addix!"

"I have another task in mind for your team," Bethany Anne told them firmly. "Gödel is mine, and mine alone."

Alexis was about to argue further when Gabriel stayed her with a hand. "What task?"

"You'll find out," Bethany Anne promised. "Just as soon as we arrive at the *Meredith Reynolds*."

AUTHOR NOTES - N.D. ROBERTS

DECEMBER 5, 2019

Hello again! Of course, I want to start by thanking you for reading all the way to my waffly wafflings. I don't know what a creative mind would do without you to demand...I mean, ask ever so nicely for more books... Let's be honest, demanding is a much more appropriate description with a bunch of book addicts like us—and as an author, I'm all too happy to oblige.

I'm feeling quite introspective as I write these notes, no doubt as a result of it being my last week in the US for this year. Life in the Stiegler household runs on its own time, although I'm anticipating the return to normality when I get back to the UK.

HUGE thanks to Lynne for her beautiful edit, and to the Beta and JIT teams for their effort in making this book all shiny in post-production. I appreciate you all SO much!

While I'm on the subject, I have to thank Marc Stiegler *enormously* for his insights into how technology works. The final scenes are much richer for our long conversations about how hacking, and his guidance on my research was invaluable. How many authors have access to the fine mind of someone whose life's work helped shape the world as we know it? I'm incredibly blessed to call him family. (Read his Braintrust series if you haven't already! I promise you won't be able to put it down!)

This is the conclusion of *Out of Time*, but you will be able to find my next Kurtherian project, titled *Queen of the Mad*, very soon. I am determined that the Sarah Jennifer Walton story will be in the store by the end of Spring, 2020. Those who follow my author page on Facebook know that the project has taken a while to get through development, since it has all the answers to the burning questions everyone has about the Age of Madness while wrapping in canon from TKG, the Second Dark Age, the Age of Expansion, and the Age of Magic. Nobody said it would be an easy project, but it's become the one that speaks most to my heart as an author and I'm writing furiously to get it to you!

And so, I return Alexis and Gabriel to their rightful place by Bethany Anne's side. It's been a lot of fun chasing these teenagers into maturity, although I can promise you that their lessons in life are not done with entirely!

I leave you with this poem by another fine mind as a final goodbye for the series.

Kahlil Gibran - 1883-1931

And a woman who held a babe against her bosom said, Speak to us of Children.
And he said:
Your children are not your children.

They are the sons and daughters of Life's longing for itself.
They come through you but not from you,
And though they are with you yet they belong not to you.
You may give them your love but not your thoughts,
For they have their own thoughts.
You may house their bodies but not their souls,
For their souls dwell in the house of tomorrow, which you
cannot visit, not even in your dreams.
You may strive to be like them, but seek not to make them
like you.
For life goes not backward nor tarries with yesterday.
You are the bows from which your children as living arrows
are sent forth.
The archer sees the mark upon the path of the infinite, and He
bends you with His might that His arrows may go swift and far.
Let your bending in the archer's hand be for gladness;
For even as He loves the arrow that flies, so He loves also the
bow that is stable.

Ad aeternitatem, until we meet again,
Nat

WOOT! Thank you for reading through both the story and all the way back through the *Author Notes*.

So, Judith and I were blessed to be hosted at Marc and Lynne's home on a trip back to Texas (we were selling our house there.)

They live on a quiet piece of property not that far from the freeway in a small town surrounded by mountains. When you head east not that far, you find additional beautiful mountains, and I can understand why they chose the idyllic life they lead.

With many dogs (not understanding that part, but then I'm still too close to empty nest just happening.) (*Editor's note: Only four, Michael. That's not a lot. Is it? Michael?*)

Both of them worked for many, many years with companies (HP / Autodesk, for example) that have changed the world, and through products (instead of actors), I have my own version of six degrees of separation.

I have, for instance, made my livelihood by using an Autodesk product (AutoCAD) and owned HP machines in my life. I never would have thought I'd know people who were instrumental in those companies.

You see, at that time (90s) I lived in Houston, TX, and Compaq Computers (NW of Houston) and Dell (Austin) were the companies I was most familiar with. I had no concept of going to California in my future.

Life has a way of bringing great friends into your orbit.

I can say that Bethany Anne brought the four of us (Lynne / Nat / Marc & me) into orbit, and I'm just amazed how Lynne and Marc have damn near become Nat's American mom and dad when she is from the UK.

All through the power of books and readers.

So thank you for reading our stories. Because of you, new families are being made worldwide.

Ad Aeternitatem,

Michael Anderle

Available Now at your Favorite e-book retailer

Two Rebels whose Worlds Collide on a Planetary Level.

On the fringes of human space, a murder will light a fuse and send two different people colliding together.

She lives on Earth, where peace among the population is a given. He is on the fringe of society where authority is how much firepower you wield.

She is from the powerful, the elite. He is with the military.

Both want the truth – but is revealing the truth good for society?

Two years ago, a small moon in a far off system was set to be the location of the first intergalactic war between humans and an alien race.

It never happened. However, something was found many are willing to kill to keep a secret.

Now, they have killed the wrong people.

How many will need to die to keep the truth hidden?

As many as is needed.

He will have vengeance no matter the cost. *She will dig for the truth. No matter how risky the truth is to reveal.*

CONNECT WITH MICHAEL ANDERLE

Michael Anderle Social
  Website:
  http://www.lmbpn.com

Email List:
  http://lmbpn.com/email/

Facebook Here:
  www.facebook.com/TheKurtherianGambitBooks/